I0757961

THE DARKEST WITCH

RITE WORLD: VAMPIRE WARS BOOK 2

JULIANA HAYGERT

COPYRIGHT

This book is a work of fiction. Names, characters, places, and incidents either are products of the author's imagination or are used fictitiously. Any resemblance to actual persons, living or dead, events, or locales is entirely coincidental.

Copyright © 2021 by Juliana Haygert

All rights reserved. This book or any portion thereof may not be reproduced or used in any manner whatsoever without the express written permission of the publisher except for the use of brief quotations in a book review.

Manufactured in the United States of America.

First Edition December 2021

www.JulianaHaygert.com

Edited by H. Danielle Crabtree

Proofread by Jessica Nelson

Cover design by Moorbooks Design

Any trademark, service marks, product names, or names featured are the property of their respective owners, and are used only for reference. There is no implied endorsement if one of these terms is used.

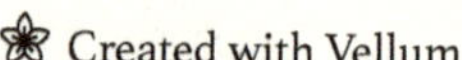 Created with Vellum

AUTHOR'S NOTE

I hope you enjoy reading *The Darkest Witch*!

Don't forget to sign up for my Newsletter to find out about new releases, cover reveals, giveaways, and more!

If you want to see exclusive teasers, help me decide on covers, read excerpts, talk about books, etc, join my reader group on Facebook: Juliana's Club!

Welcome to the RITE WORLD!

Free Novella:
The Vampire Hunt

Novellas:
The Hunter Path
The Light Calling
The Light Witch

Rite World:
The Vampire Heir (Book 1)
The Witch Queen (Book 2)
The Immortal Vow (Book 3)
The Warlock Lord (Book 4)
The Wolf Consort (Book 5)
The Crystal Rose (Book 6)
The Wolf Forsaken (Book 7)
The Fae Bound (Book 8)
The Blood Pact (Book 9)

Rite World: Blackthorn Hunters Academy
The Demons Kiss (Book 1)
The Hunter Secret (Book 2)
The Soul Bond (Book 3)
The Shadow Trials (Book 4)
The Immortal Vow (Book 5)

Rite World: Lightgrove Witches
The Midnight Test (Book 1)
The Midnight Spell (Book 2)
The Midnight Flame (Book 3)

Rite World: Vampire Wars
The Darkest Vampire (Book 1)
The Darkest Witch (Book 2)
The Darkest Magic (Book 3)

And more to come!

1

I grunted. "Easier said than done."

Killian feinted to the right and I almost fell for it. We circled each other, our hands raised, our knees bent, and our boots crunching the grass underneath.

Not long ago, Killian had offered to teach me how to use my dagger and defend myself. So, for the last two evenings, after a long day of driving, we walked to the nearest park or wooded area, usually located behind the inn we had stopped at, and he demonstrated fighting moves and then asked me to show him what I learned.

"Just roll them. Like this." He rolled his shoulders.

I fought the urge to avert my eyes. If I took my eyes off him, he would attack and I wouldn't have time to react. But it was increasingly hard to look at him.

Killian wore a T-shirt that clung to his powerful torso, and the fact that he had folded up the short sleeves, showing off the muscles in his arms and shoulders, didn't help a bit. The dark pants weren't any better, hugging his strong thighs and round ass. The dying sun shone down on us and gave his light-brown hair a golden gleam. I knew he was a vampire, more similar to a demon than anything else, but there were plenty of moments when I thought he had to be related to a god.

Were there gods and goddesses in the supernatural world? There were vampires, werewolves, fae, witches ... why not gods?

Shaking my head, I rolled my shoulders. "I'm trying."

But it was hard. Because he was handsome, hot, and I was nervous I would mess things up; I really sucked at this. Despite this being only our second training session, I was absolutely sure I hadn't been born for combat fighting. With a sigh, I stopped and put my hands on my waist.

"We should give up."

It didn't matter I was half demon hunter and was supposed to have slightly increased strength, agility, and stamina—more than a human, a lot less than a vampire. It was like the demon hunter genes didn't want anything to do with me.

"Lavinia," Killian whispered. His shoulders straightened, bringing him to his full height. He was almost an entire head taller than me. "I know you don't like this, but it's important. You know what happened with the demon hunters. They—"

"They had something that neutralized my powers, I remember." Not that my magic was of much help. Although, when the demon hunters had Killian, Delia, and me cornered, the blood promise would have let me do something.

He stepped closer. "If you can't use your powers, you need to be able to at least break free from whoever is holding you and run."

And that was another reason this was hard. How could I learn how to fight under such pressure? A group of demons knew about the box and they wanted it ... and me.

Paranoia nagged at me, and the urge to look over my shoulder hit me again.

If I was any good at fighting, then maybe I had a chance. But an invisible clock ticked over my head, counting down to when they would come for me. I didn't have time to get good at fighting. What I needed was to break the blood promise—but that was also impossible.

Damn, my life was complicated.

"Hopefully, that won't happen again," I muttered.

"I hope so too." Killian inched closer. "I hope we get to DuMoir Castle before anyone else finds us ... finds you and the box, but we need to be prepared."

Another step.

Now I could see the faint marks of the scars lining his arms. His entire body was covered in those scars, most faint, but a handful were really red and angry. He had gotten them when he was inside the box, but he shut down my other questions about it. Those memories were too painful.

I wanted to tell him to put on his jacket, or at least wear long sleeves like me. It was the middle of October, but we had been sticking to the upper part of the United States for our road trip, where the temperatures were getting chillier by the day. But he was a freaking vampire and the cold didn't bother him at all.

Me, on the other hand. I smoothed my hands over my arms, clad in a thick thermal tee. "Maybe we should change plans, then. Instead of training in the evenings, we should stop around noon, train first, have lunch, and then hit the road again. At least it won't be this cold."

Yes, it was cold, but I was stalling. I didn't want to practice, period.

"We can do that, but since we are here, give me thirty more minutes," he said, his naturally rough voice filling the space between us. "Then we can call it a night."

I stared into his eyes. Those brilliant, deep green eyes. Why did he have to be so handsome? And why had he kissed me and then acted as if nothing had happened? When he invited me to DuMoir Castle with him, I thought things had changed. I thought he was finally surrendering to whatever was going on between us, but now I was his partner. Before, our goal had been to find the killers who were ravaging the supernatural community. Now our goal was to get to DuMoir Castle, located in the Northeast, safely.

What happened after?

"All right," I said, unhappy but eager to get this over with.

Killian retreated. Hands up hovered at chest level, his legs angled shoulder-width apart, and his knees bent slightly—loose for movement, but a strong foundation. With an exhale, I rolled my shoulders and mirrored his stance.

Relax, I told myself. I had to relax.

Once more, Killian feinted to the right. I didn't fall for it. But then he feinted left, and I did. I prepared for his attack, but it didn't come as I expected. Killian turned to the right again and practically barreled into my side. With a grunt, I raised my arms, blocking his fists. I hissed as the pain of the impact reverberated through my arms. He threw his leg out in a beautiful sequence of kicks, and I blocked all of them but the last one, which hit me right in my side. But he didn't apologize or slow down. Groaning, I ducked below a punch and twirled out of the way.

Or tried to.

My foot got caught on a rock protruding from the earth. I tripped, bracing myself against the impact my back and shoulders were about to sustain, but an arm snaked around my waist, stopping my momentum and smoothing my landing. I lay on the cold grass, with Killian's arm securely around me and his body hovering a few inches over mine.

I stopped breathing as my eyes locked with his. His gaze darkened, his jaw tightened, and his entire body radiated power and tension. Suddenly, I wasn't cold anymore. I held still, afraid that if I moved or breathed, Killian would break the spell. That he would pull away, like he had done before.

But he stayed above me, immobile and rigid, his eyes searching mine. My fingers itched to reach to him, to touch him, to graze the five o'clock shadow on his chin and jaw, to sink into his silky hair. I wanted to arch my back, to raise my head, to bring my lips to his. I desired to feel his lips on mine again, to taste him, to explore every inch of his body.

His gaze slid down to my lips and I inhaled deeply. This was it. He would kiss me again.

Then his eyes moved down, to my throat.

Of course, my blood was more alluring than my kisses.

Coldness fell over me as Killian disappeared.

One second, he was on top of me. The next, I was staring at the darkening sky.

I sat up and found him several feet away.

He ran a hand over his hair. "Are ... are you okay?"

I frowned. He couldn't have helped me up? I pushed up to my feet and patted the grass from my pants. "I'm fine," I snapped.

"Then ... we can stop for today." His eyes hardened. "I'm going ..." He pointed to the woods at my back.

He was going feeding. That had been clear when he

stared at my neck. He did that often, which should worry me more than it did.

"Sure," I said, hoping my voice didn't betray how disappointed I was. Disappointed at being only a meal he couldn't have. Nothing more.

He gestured to the building peeking from above a line of trees to our left. "You should go back to our room. Make sure you bolt the door. I'll bring you some takeout when I get back."

I opened my mouth to tell him I could find food myself, but then he was gone. I barely saw as he zipped into the woods and disappeared again.

Letting out a breath, I dragged my feet back to the inn.

2

THERE WERE MOMENTS WHEN I MISSED FOREST CREEK. IT HAD been hard to part ways with all that was familiar to me.

It took me almost two weeks to pack, move all of my things to Delia's house—*my* house—and return my apartment to its owner early, though I ended up paying the full lease. I locked the house but left a key with Suzie, so she could stop by every couple of months to make sure everything was all right.

That had been hard too. Saying goodbye to Suzie and the tea shop. I told her I hoped it was a temporary thing, but I had gotten news of some relatives—a lie, but what else was I supposed to tell her? That I was half witch, half demon hunter and that I had opened a magical box, let out a vampire, and now demons were after the box and me?

If all worked out, Lord Drake would know what to do with the box. Breaking my connection to the box would hopefully make whoever was after me stop, and then I would be able to go back to my normal life.

I wasn't even sure I wanted that, but it was all I had.

Arriving at the inn, I ambled up the stairs to the second floor, my feet rattling the metal railings with each impact against the concrete steps. On the second floor, doors lined one side, while a short rail protected travelers from toppling into the parking lot below. My beat-up Corolla looked small and pathetic nestled between two large black SUVs.

After entering our room, my fingers twisted the lock.

The instant I turned around, it hit me. The box's pull. It had increased exponentially since I used it to escape the demon hunters' trap, and now its presence called to me.

Killian said the pull he felt was a painful thing, tugging at his soul, wanting it, consuming it.

For me, it was different. Its allure, its enchanting call, sang like a siren. The feeling, the tug, promised rewards, pleasure, and paradise.

But mostly power.

The taste of the box's power still lingered, and my body craved more.

Shaking off the allure, I grabbed clean clothes from the bag I left beside my bed. I did my best to ignore the box, which was wrapped in a small hand towel, inside a duffel bag, tucked inside the closet.

Out of sight. Out of mind.

I glanced at the second bed and Killian's bag. He had insisted we sleep in the same room for safety. In case someone attacked in the middle of the night. But damn, seeing him sleeping just a few feet from me—everything was hard with him.

I plopped down on my bed, suddenly exhausted. Losing Delia, leaving Forest Creek and Suzie's Brew behind, being chased by demons, putting up with a brooding Killian, feeling the box's pull, and still not being able to access my full magic had left me mentally and physically drained.

Curling into a fetal position wouldn't fix anything. With a sigh, I rose, a painful tug tweaking my lower back. Cursing, I went to the bathroom and lifted my shirt in front of the mirror. A pink bruise spread on the side of my waist and lower back—where Killian had kicked me during practice.

Shit, this was nasty, and it was starting to hurt like a bitch.

I kept my shirt folded over my breasts, my midriff exposed, and went back to my bed, where I dug into my supply bag for my herbs. I could make a salve to apply to the bruise so it wouldn't be too bad, and I could make a potion for the pain.

I put the herbs aside and was fishing out the only mortar and pestle I had brought, when the bedroom's door opened and Killian walked in, carrying a McDonald's takeout bag.

He froze, his gaze locked on my stomach. Then, his brows slammed down and he lifted his eyes to meet mine. "I hurt you." He closed the door and took two steps in.

I shrugged, suddenly self-conscious over my state of undress. I ignored the urge to shrink away. "Isn't that supposed to happen during training?"

"I was holding back," he said, his voice rougher than usual. "I was holding *a lot* back. And I still hurt you."

"It's okay." I held the mortar and pestle up. "I can fix it."

He stared at me, at the mortar and pestle, at the herbs on my bed, at my bare stomach. His eyes darkened and his jaw ticked with tension; he squeezed the top of the takeout bag until I thought it would rip.

With a grunt, he dropped the bag on his bed. "Your dinner."

Then, he turned to the door.

I gawked at his back. "Where are you going?"

"I just ... I need some fresh air."

And just like that, he was gone.

What the hell was that?

My head swirled with a million thoughts; my chest constricted with my held breath. What was wrong with him?

What was wrong with me?

No, I wouldn't go down that road, because I couldn't begin to comprehend how Killian felt. He had always hated witches, but I thought that after what we went through together, after I freed him from the box, after we exacted revenge for our families, after our kiss, that things had changed between us. Maybe he didn't hate witches anymore, or at least he didn't hate me. I thought he felt the same attraction I did, especially when he had been the one to invite me to come with him. I was here because he had brought me with him.

Irritated, I hopped into the shower. The hot water relaxed my sore muscles, but didn't ease the hunger gnarling at the pit of my stomach. After the shower, I quickly ate while I finished the salve and the tonic. I smoothed the salve over the surface of the bruise, wrapped it with a bandage so it wouldn't get my pajamas dirty, and settled into bed.

Watching the door. Waiting.

Where had Killian gone? Why wasn't he here? Did he hate me so much he couldn't stand to be near me?

I wanted to pretend I didn't care, but the longing I felt called me a liar. I was hopeless.

Sitting with my back against the headboard, I turned on the TV, putting on a random movie. The tonic's relaxing properties kicked in, and my eyelids drooped, heavy with sleep. I turned off the TV, snuggled into the bed, hugged one of the pillows, and closed my eyes.

I WOKE UP WITH A START, my body immobilized. Killian's body was flush with mine, his mouth an inch from mine. His musky scent wrapped around me like an inebriating drug. My heart went into overdrive. Had he changed his mind about me?

My hands shoved at his chest, but he didn't move. Instead, he placed a finger over his lips. Leaning into me, he placed his mouth next to my ear.

Oh, my Lord …

"We've been found," he whispered. I stilled. "A dozen people are searching the inn." He touched his lips to my ears. "When I say so, I need you to get your things and run."

"But—"

Pulling back, he stared at me, his eyes cold as ice. "No buts. Just do what I say."

Killian was the trained soldier here, the one with battle experience. I nodded.

For twelve torturous seconds, we didn't move. We barely breathed, but I could feel his entire body against mine, I could see the way he looked at me, his eyes searching mine, and I liked the way his hands splayed beside my head, caging me in.

He shot to his feet, pulling me with him. "Now!"

I sprang into action, grabbing my bag and shoving my boots on.

Not a second later, the door burst open. My heart hammered against my chest.

Killian bared his fangs, ready to attack.

Three men wearing long cloaks walked in.

And Killian faltered.

"What—?"

One of the men curled his lips. "Surprised to see me, Killian?"

I gaped at them.

Killian recovered and snarled. "Tack. Whatever you're here for, you're wasting your time."

"Is that the way you greet an old friend?"

Killian scoffed. "You and the other warlocks kidnapped me. You kept me sedated for weeks, and then helped Soren put me in the box. We're *not* friends."

Oh, shit. These were warlocks, and apparently, the exact ones who had captured Killian twenty years ago. The ones who had created the boxes.

The box!

With trembling hands, I grabbed the bag with the box from inside the closet and hugged it tight.

"It's all about perspective." Tack took a step closer, clearly not afraid of Killian. "I sent you friends to invite you back, but you killed them. Not very nice of you."

"The demons," I whispered.

Tack glanced past Killian and smiled wider at me. "Exactly. You must be the girl who can open the box. I've been looking for you."

I retreated a step, every muscle in my body shaking.

Killian shifted so he was right in front of me. "I'll give you ten seconds to leave."

Tack laughed. "What? Do you think you can escape? Over a dozen warlocks are waiting for you to try."

I remembered the talisman the demon hunters had. It

inhibited any supernatural's powers. I just hoped these warlocks didn't have anything like that, or we would be in big trouble. Well, even bigger.

Killian's body blurred as he assaulted the warlocks. Magic bolts soared at Killian, striking the walls, lamps, and furniture in the wake of his vampire speed. Two warlocks went down. Killian backhanded Tack, throwing him aside like a fly. The warlock hit the wall and crumpled to his knees.

Killian grabbed his bag from the bed and offered me his hand. "Come."

I slid my hand into his.

As he pulled me toward the door, I glanced at Tack. He pushed up to his feet and conjured a big bolt between his hands. He threw it.

"Killian!" I screamed. Without thinking, I threw my body in front of Killian and extended my arms out. A thin wall of blue light appeared as a bolt hit it, throwing me backward. The barrier crumbled.

Killian steadied me. "What the ...?"

I mimicked Tack's hands curled around one another and a big blue ball of magic appeared. I threw it at him, hitting him square in the chest. This time, he went down and stayed down.

I gaped at my hands, bemused by my instincts.

Killian grabbed my hand again. "No time to marvel. We need to go."

We ran out of the room, and sure enough, warlocks closed in on us from both sides.

Killian locked his arm around my waist and held me tight. "Hang on."

He jumped off the rail.

I inhaled deeply, a scream lodged in my throat. My stomach dipped and I thought I would lose my dinner.

Then, we were on the ground, and he set my feet down but didn't let go of my hand.

"You have nowhere to run!" someone yelled behind us as bolts of magic rained down on us.

Killian ran with me, faster than I could ever do by myself, but not his usual fast. In a blur, he opened my car's door and pushed me inside. He followed. The bolts hit the car like bullets, sizzling and smoking on contact. The engine revved to life, and we raced out of the parking lot.

I glanced back at the inn as we hit the road, hard and fast, and saw the warlocks gathered in the parking lot. At least a dozen of them.

My stomach knotted.

I sat straighter, looking at Killian.

Now didn't seem like a good time to ask him about Tack. Though, I couldn't help but panic. If these warlocks found us —the same warlocks who had started this mess twenty years ago—who said they couldn't find us again?

We were doomed.

3

We drove for several hours nonstop. When we finally stopped, it was for him to feed while I got breakfast from a roadside gas station.

And to switch cars.

As much as I hated it, Killian compelled a guy to switch cars with us and forget everything about it. We went north. A couple of hours later, we stopped and did it again. This time, we drove east. Then we did again, and went south.

For twenty-four hours, Killian only stopped to get food for me and switch cars, hoping to lose whoever was tracking us.

The first couple of hours in the car had been tense. I was sure the warlocks were following us, and the way Killian gripped the wheel and kept the car steady at an incredible speed didn't help.

But after the third car and direction change, I was tired, grumpy, and plain bored. I ended up sleeping most of the zigzag trip.

When I woke up the next morning, the sun was rising over snowcapped mountains.

"Where are we?" I asked, straightening in my seat. This time, Killian had gotten a Range Rover, and it was incredibly comfortable and full of fancy, high-end tech.

"Canada," he said. "North of Prince Albert."

I stared at him. "We crossed the Canadian border? How?"

Killian spared one quick, bored glance at me. Of course. Compulsion. How else?

His shoulders had relaxed for the first time since the attack at the inn. "I'm sure you have questions."

"I do, but I can't wait until you're ready."

"I might never be ready. And right now, we have nothing else to do other than driving."

I frowned. "And then what? We'll switch cars and direction again?"

"Probably."

"It'll take weeks for us to get to the East Coast this way."

"Better than being captured. Next time, it won't be a dozen warlocks. It'll be fifty. And I don't think we can run from fifty warlocks."

"So ..." I was really curious, but I was afraid of opening old wounds. "Those were Soren's warlocks?"

Eyes on the road, Killian nodded. "I'm guessing that warlock who overthrew Soren ... what was his name?"

"Keeran," I said. Delia had mentioned him, although she didn't know details.

"Right. Keeran." He glanced at me, at the bag at my feet—the box. "It has been twenty years, and they are as invested in the boxes as they were before. They won't stop coming after it. After you."

I clicked my tongue. "Tack knew I could open the box. How?"

"I don't know, though I'm sure that's why they are after you." He paused. "I wonder what happened to Acalla. If she was still with them, then they wouldn't need you."

"Maybe she ran away, like Delia did."

"Or Soren finally killed her."

"But didn't he love her?"

"Soren was insane. Even if he loved her, she wasn't safe with him."

And there was the kid too. When Delia ran with the boxes, Acalla had a toddler son, Esmund. Was he safe with his father? I hoped he hadn't killed them. I hoped he hadn't killed anyone else, though from the tales I had heard from Delia and Killian, that seemed unlikely.

I shrank in the seat. I was tired of this mess. Sometimes I wished I could just give the box to Killian and tell him to take it to DuMoir Castle by himself. But now that the warlocks knew I could open the box, would they leave me alone?

I was tied to this fate, no matter how much I wanted to change it.

"Are you hungry?" Killian asked.

I pressed a hand to my stomach. I didn't even remember the last time I ate, or what I ate. "It's breakfast time," I told him.

He nodded.

There was a small town at the next exit and we stopped at a quaint diner. While I went in and got us a table, Killian went scouting. He was too wired and wanted to make sure there was no one suspicious around the diner. Or the several blocks around it.

I ordered a healthy plate of scrambled eggs, bacon, and

toast; a mug of tea for me; and some coffee for Killian. I was halfway through my plate when he showed up.

"Sorry." He sat across from me and leaned over the table. "I saw a deer in a wooded area and ..."

He didn't need to finish. Oh, lord. The bite I had in my mouth soured, but I forced it down. I had to eat, even if I had lost my appetite. But it was hard to push it down. It took longer than I wanted, but finally, I finished it all.

Impatience shone in Killian's eyes when I pushed my empty plate to the side.

"I'm ready," I told him.

"Maybe you should order something to go," he said. "So we don't need to stop for lunch."

That was a good idea, but did he expect me to stay in the car for hours and not stretch my legs? And what about peeing? He might not have that problem, but I did.

I stood up. "We can stop by some fast-food joint and order at the drive-thru."

I turned to go to the counter and pay, and ended up bumping my arm into someone's. A jolt raced through my skin, raising the hairs on my arms.

"Whoa," the someone said.

I looked up at the girl in front of me. She was beautiful with long, dark-brown hair, tanned skin, and round chocolate eyes.

"You felt that?"

"It was quite the shock," she said, amused. She smiled at the guy beside her—a tall young man with brown hair and blue eyes. He was just as beautiful as she was. "Sorry about that."

"It's okay. I was the one who bumped into you."

Killian stood by my side and together, we went to the

counter, where I paid for the meal in cash. We exited the diner and walked the short distance to our car across the street.

But Killian didn't unlock the doors. He stood beside the car, his head low.

I rounded the car and walked to him. "What is it?"

"I hear something ..." He closed his eyes, focusing. "Voices, a strange language." He paused. "They are hiding, around the diner."

My eyes bugged. "More warlocks? Do you think they found us?"

"I don't know ..." He looked up, at a narrow alley two stores from the diner. Then his gaze shifted to the corner on the other side. "They are moving."

A second later, ten figures emerged in black pants, shirts, vests, and wearing long red cloaks with hoods that concealed their faces. As a swarm, they entered the diner.

"They think we're still in there," I said, watching in horror. "We should go. Before they realize we're not there."

"No, I don't think they are here for you." Killian stared at the diner.

I turned and watched it too.

From the large glass windows, we could see the people inside the diner screaming and running. Most of them made it out.

Except for that couple.

Cornered by the hooded men, the girl picked up several vials from the slim belt around her waist and the guy held up a sword—where had that come from? The girl smiled as she threw a couple of vials at the hooded men. Dark smoke swirled around them. When the smoke faded, three hooded men were down.

"She's a witch," I whispered, stunned. And just like me, she was good with potions. I ran toward the diner.

"Lavinia!" Killian called out.

I fished the dagger from inside my boot and joined the fray. "Hey, stupid!" I called at the men's back. Two of them turned to me. When they came for me, I let myself grow scared—it was the only way to activate my magic. I released a blue bolt at one, and Killian took care of the second one. He snapped the man's neck like a twig.

I felt both disgust for the way he handled this and pride that he had joined me.

Killian and I handled two more, until all ten hooded men were at our feet, either dead or unconscious. My stomach recoiled at the thought, but I held on to it. I didn't push it away; I didn't ignore it. Death would never be easy or okay, but it seemed to be a big part of my life now. The sooner I got used to people dying like that, the better.

The girl looked at me. "A witch." She glanced at Killian. "And a vampire. I like it."

I frowned. "You're a witch too."

She nodded. "Yes. It's a little complicated, but yeah, I am."

What could be complicated about being a witch? Regardless, she was the first witch close to my age that I had met, and for some reason that made me more excited than it should.

"I'm Lavinia." I gestured to the vampire. "And this is Killian."

With that same stoic and dangerous mien from when I first met him, Killian dipped his chin.

"Cool." The girl picked up a bottle from the floor that hadn't broken. "I'm Evelyn."

Then the guy said, "I'm Asher."

4

"WHO WERE THESE MEN?" KILLIAN TOED ONE OF THE BODIES. "I've never seen anyone like them before."

"These were members of the Brotherhood of Purity," Asher said. "They hunt witches."

My eyes widened. "You mean like the Lightgrove coven?"

Evelyn and Asher exchanged a glance.

"If you don't know about the Brotherhood, how do you know about the Lightgrove witches?" Evelyn asked.

"I went to New Orleans a couple of weeks ago to ask for their help, and—"

"Wait," Asher said. He glanced past our backs. "Hm, we have a problem."

We spun around and sure enough, there were half a dozen people outside the window, some taking pictures, others calling who knows what.

"You guys clean up in here," Killian said. "I'll take care of them."

He marched out and called out to the people to gather around him. Meanwhile, Evelyn, Asher, and I cleaned up the mess—or rather, I watched as Evelyn and Asher moved around each other like a well-oiled machine. Asher moved the bodies to the back, and Evelyn retrieved vials from her utility belt and threw them on the floor. The blood staining the tiles evaporated instantly. And I used a broom to sweep the broken glasses and plates to a pile. I transferred them to a trash bag and took it to the back.

Soon, the place was almost like before, sans a few glasses and plates. The staff returned as if nothing had happened, and patrons came in too.

"Would you help me with the bodies?" Asher asked Killian when he came back in.

He glanced at me and I gave him a short nod. "Sure," he told Asher through gritted teeth. He wasn't happy about this, but he did it anyway.

Both of them disappeared into the back.

"Your vampire doesn't seem too happy," Evelyn said.

"Oh, hm, he's not *my* vampire," I said, way too quickly.

Evelyn lifted an eyebrow but didn't push it. She turned to the counter. "What do you say we order some coffee and sit outside to talk?"

"I would like that, but only if I can have tea instead."

"Tea?" Evelyn looked at me as if I was crazy. "All right, then."

<hr>

THE STREET CORNER had a big open area with wooden benches, in front of a closed store. Evelyn and I sat on one of the benches with our coffee and tea.

The bench was cold and I shivered. It was mid-morning and the sun had just now started warming up the day.

"So you know the Lightgrove witches?" Evelyn asked.

I nodded. "I went to them to ask for help."

"For ...?"

I sighed. "Well, my magic is limited, and I thought they could help me figure out why and maybe get it back." I didn't want to get into details with her. Not yet, at least. "How about you?"

Evelyn stared at her coffee. "I was born a light witch, like the Lightgrove coven, but my magic manifested like a dark witch." Oh, shit, that didn't sound good. "I was hunted by dark and light witches alike, and also by the Brotherhood."

"I know how that feels. My parents were killed by demon hunters when I was eleven. I was alone for several years then."

"Wow, at eleven. That must have been hard."

It was, but I didn't want to talk about that. "How did you meet Asher?"

A smile graced her lips. "Asher is actually the son of a dark witch." My mouth formed a round O. Evelyn chuckled. "I know. It was unexpected. With light and dark witches, the male passes on the magical gene, but it doesn't manifest in them. But ... you've been to the Light Castle, so you know about the Light Order."

"I just saw they are a bunch of warriors."

"They are the husbands, lovers, and sons of witches, the ones who wanted to be involved in their lives and protect them."

"That's amazing!"

"It is, but the dark witches have the same idea," Evelyn said. "Asher's mother wanted to create her own Dark Order and have Asher as the captain. But Asher was wise enough to see how evil his mother was. He had no interest in joining her. Anyway, Asher and I met when he was running from her."

"Like it was meant to be."

A soft grin adorned Evelyn's lips. "How about you and the vampire?"

How much could I tell her? She seemed trustworthy. "I ended up helping him with a spell, without meaning to. Then he stuck around because there were some demon hunters killing supernaturals, though at the time we didn't know who was behind the murders." I waved my hands. "Anyway, I still have my magic blocked, so he's taking me to his coven. The lord of his coven is mated to a powerful witch. I'm hoping she can help me." That wasn't a total lie, though I hadn't told her the true reason we were heading to DuMoir Castle.

"Ah, okay." She sounded disappointed.

"What is it?"

"Asher and I are tracking some dark witches who live in the area," she said. "I believe they have dragon bones."

My eyes widened. "Dragon? As in, like ... dragons are real?"

"They used to be. As far as I know, they've been extinct for centuries now."

"What a shame. It would be cool to meet a dragon."

"And dangerous! They were powerful and moody beings. Anyway, once a dragon dies, most of their magic is stored in their bones and teeth, and some witches can control that magic." She gestured to herself. "That's a dark witch magic. A dangerous magic. I've been collecting dragon bones. My plan is to take them to the Light Castle so the Lightgrove witches can safely store them away from anyone who might want to use that power for evil."

It sounded like Killian and me with the box. We had one, and hoped it stayed that way, but we were taking it to someone who would know what to do with it. I hoped.

"I think you're doing a good thing."

"Right? I think so too. Just these Brotherhood pests. The zealots are good at tracking witches. Anyway ..." She turned to me, a glint in her chocolate eyes. "I was wondering if you and Killian would be up to help us find the witches' place and steal the dragon bones."

"Oh." Shit. I didn't know what to think. It could be both fun and dangerous, but ... "Killian and I need to get to his coven, the sooner the better. I'm sorry."

"No worries," Evelyn said. "We had been by ourselves for a few months now, and when I saw you two, I might have gotten a little excited. The four of us fighting together would be really cool. But I understand."

As if they knew this conversation was ending, Killian and Asher walked out of an alley beside the diner and toward us.

I got up. "It was nice meeting you, Evelyn. I'm sorry we can't help you."

She stood too. "Well, if you change your mind, Asher and I will be around for a few more days, probably at the inn just outside of town." She pointed to the west. "Safe trip."

"Thanks."

Asher halted beside Evelyn, his hand immediately snaking around her waist.

Killian stopped to nudge me to follow him. I waved at Evelyn and Asher, and then went with Killian to our car. We hopped in and Killian peeled off the curb.

"Everything okay?" I asked as he drove us out of town.

Killian nodded. "Yes. We just took the bodies to the woods." As usual.

I wanted to ask Killian what he and Asher had talked about, but he was still stoic. I feared that if I pushed, he would bite me.

Literally.

I settled in the seat and got ready for the next five or so hours of driving. I was getting sick and tired of driving around like a maniac.

I closed my eyes, hoping to sleep.

A faint tug rumbled deep in my chest for a moment and then was gone. I ignored it, thinking it was indigestion and gas.

Three minutes later, it happened again, only a fraction stronger.

And then again.

And again.

I sat upright and rubbed my hand against my chest.

"Your heart is beating faster," Killian said, stealing glances at me. "What is it?"

"I feel something," I whispered, trying to focus.

The next time the sensation came, I opened up to it. It was a faint, delicious pull, a call of allure and desire and need, of infinite power, of impossible promises, and enticing—

I gasped.

Killian pulled the car over and stopped at the road's shoulder. "What is it?"

"I ... I feel it."

"Feel what?"

I stared at Killian as the sensation came back, and this time, I was so attuned to it, I could even tell where it was coming from. "A box."

5

───────

"WHAT DO YOU MEAN?" HE STRETCHED HIS HAND TOWARD MY legs. "The box is right there."

"No, not this one."

Killian worked his jaw. "You're saying you feel another box?"

I rubbed my chest, the pull fainter now, but still there. "I think so."

He shook his head. "How is that possible?"

"I don't know. How can I open this one?" I toed the bag at my feet. "How are the warlocks finding us? There are too many questions we don't have the answer for."

"Are ... are you sure it's a box?" He sounded irritated as if I was doing this on purpose.

"Of course I'm not sure!" My own irritation spiked. "But ... it feels like the one we have, right after I used it." And hurt him. "The box, or whatever it is, is calling me."

Killian narrowed his eyes, his knuckles white around the wheel. "I don't like this."

"Me neither, but I don't think we should ignore it." I pressed my lips tight before continuing. "I don't know why, but I think that this box is also exposed and that's why I can feel it." If it had been discovered, the box would be out in the open, without Delia's wards to muffle its powers. "If someone has this box ..."

Killian exhaled. "That's dangerous."

"Exactly. If someone has this box, they could use it for evil." And I knew firsthand how the box's magic could corrupt one's mind and soul. Even if a person didn't mean to be evil, they would turn out that way after consuming the box's magic. I was sure of that. "We have to go after it."

"What if it isn't the box? Or if it's still buried?"

"Then we leave," I said simply. "If it's not the box, then it doesn't matter to us. If it is the box and it's buried, we memorize its place, and take this one to DuMoir Castle, and talk to Lord Drake and Queen Thea to decide what to do with it." I wanted to break the connection I had with the boxes and be done with them.

"And what if it is the box and someone else has it?"

"We take it." It was safer this way.

Killian glanced back to the road beside us, to the bright blue sky above us, dotted with a handful of white, fluffy clouds. In the distance, snowcapped mountains shone silver in the sunlight. It was a beautiful day, albeit cold.

And now it would become colder ...

"All right, we go check it out." He faced me, his green eyes fierce. "Recon only. If it's buried, we leave it. If it's not ... we'll reassess. Deal?"

I dipped my chin once. "Deal."

"Then, tell me where to go."

I closed my eyes, let out a long breath, and focused on the feeling inside my chest. It was tingly now, and felt more like an elastic band, tightening and loosening every so often. I shook my shoulders and relaxed, filling my mind with thoughts of the elastic band. I closed a hand around the invisible elastic and pulled.

"Keep going on this road," I said, my eyes still closed.

The car rumbled underneath me as Killian brought it back to the road.

A few minutes later, I pointed to the left. "This way."

Killian cursed under his breath. "Are you spying?"

I opened my eyes. "No, why?" Then I saw the narrow road to the left. "Oh."

"Well, it's working. Keep going."

I shut my eyes again and focused on the elastic tug. For thirty minutes, we drove slowly, following the pull through narrow roads that led up the mountain. I spied from under my lashes here and there, and became wary of the overgrown vegetation flanking the rough road.

"This road hadn't been used much," Killian said at some point. "I don't have a good feeling about this."

Me neither.

Finally, the pull intensified, robbing me of air.

And then it died.

I snapped my eyes open. "It's gone."

"That must be the reason." Killian pointed to the horizon, where a big wooden ski lodge seemed carved out of the mountain. Below the lodge, rusty ski lifts and abandoned ski slopes molded around the mountain.

The road wound for at least a quarter of a mile until it led to broken metal gates that opened on an empty and snow-covered parking lot. Killian brought the car to a stop before we reached the gates.

"It looks abandoned." I leaned forward, trying to get a better look at the place.

One of the outside doors of the lodge opened and someone walked out onto a balcony overlooking the slopes.

Killian maneuvered the car so it was out of the road and under the cover of the trees. "What now?"

"We should get closer. See if this person has the box." Or find out what had called me here.

Without waiting for Killian's opinion, I picked up my leather jacket from the backseat and exited the car.

Three seconds later, Killian stood by my side, wearing only his thin suede jacket and a T-shirt. It looked great on him, I had to give him that.

"We should be careful where we step." Killian pointed down. "The layer of snow seems thicker around the lodge and we shouldn't leave footprints."

"Right." I hadn't thought about that.

We made our way forward, being careful to stick under the almost leafless trees, where there was almost no snow, and then glued to the fence, so our footprints would be hidden.

As silently as we could, we rounded the parking lot following the fence, until we were about two hundred yards from the wide wooden stairs leading to the lodge's main entrance. If we got any closer, we would have to walk in the snow, leaving our footprints behind. It was too risky.

Killian and I crouched beside the fence, three inches of snow at our feet, and peeked up.

The person on the balcony was a woman wearing a long, black gown as if she was ready to attend a ball. Her crimson hair fell into tight curls around her shoulders, and she smoked a long, thin pipe.

What was this, some kind of secret ball?

A couple of minutes later, another woman joined her. This one wore a dark blue gown and her blond hair was pulled up in an intricate bun. They faced each other and talked.

I couldn't hear them, but I knew who could. I glanced at Killian, patiently.

He lifted a finger as he listened to it.

The blonde woman screamed something. I couldn't understand her words, but even I heard that. The red-haired one turned to her, a zap of black magic flying from her fingers. The blonde waved her hand, blocking the spell.

I gasped, a little surprised, a little amused.

The two of them continued bickering as they entered the lodge once more.

"They are—"

"Witches," I whispered.

Killian nodded and gestured for us to go back the way we came. "Yes, that was clear from the spells."

I followed him. "What were they saying?"

"Nothing specific. They were arguing about some potion one of them messed up."

I frowned. "Nothing about the box?"

"Let's say they have the box; they wouldn't be talking freely about it. Besides, would they know it's a box? They might be like those demons who had mine. They might think it's a magical stone they can draw a little magic from. If they figured out even that."

True. I stared at the lodge and tried opening my senses, but there was no tug now. No call. "I can't feel it anymore."

"Does that mean it wasn't a box?"

"I'm not sure." I pressed a hand on my chest, right

between my breasts, where the sensation had come from before. "I think I don't feel it anymore because I'm right here. If we leave, the pull might come back." Or not. I was fishing for anything at this point. "Either way, we should investigate."

At the edge of the parking lot, Killian whirled and faced me. "You're suggesting we go into a den of *witches*—" I cringed at the way he said witches. "And fight them all while we look for a box that might or might not be there?"

I clenched my fists. Why was he so moody about this? I opened my mouth to yell at him when he placed a hand over my mouth, clamping my words in.

"Shhh," he whispered, before letting go of my mouth. He snaked his hand around my waist and jumped.

I swallowed a yelped and held on his shoulder when the ground faded away and a rush of air whipped my hair around. A second later, we were on the ground again, between trees, just a few yards from the fence and the gates.

My knees wobbled and my head spun. Holy shit, that had been unexpected and intense. I needed a warning!

"What was that?" I hissed as low as I could.

Killian looked around a tree and pointed to the middle of the parking lot. I looked through the other side of the same tree and inhaled deeply. A giant tiger strolled in the snow, like he owned the turf. Above him, a raven circled the sky.

"Familiars," he said.

"What?"

"Like witches' familiars. Remember the animals with Queen Denise and the council? Those were their familiars."

"And these are from these witches."

Killian nodded. "They are probably patrolling the area. There could be more. We have to be careful."

Just as he said it, the tiger stopped and his ears perked up.

We hid behind the tree again and Killian brought his finger to his lips. Shit, there was a tiger, a real, magical tiger a few yards from us. That was crazy.

"Damn," Killian whispered. Once more, he wound his arm around me and pulled me to him. "Hang on."

This time I had the warning, but it wasn't any easier.

Killian jumped up, to the top of a naked tree. Then he jumped to another tree two more times, until we were far from the parking lot. He pressed my back to the thicker trunk, his body glued to mine, his hands splayed beside my head. I was breathing hard and my heart beat way too fast from both the exhilaration of the jumps and because of him. His head almost touched mine, but his eyes scanned the trees, vegetation, and snow below, looking for more animals.

Meanwhile, I had a mini meltdown in his arms.

Didn't he know what he did to me? How he affected me? How this, having him so close, his hard body flush with mine, his scent invading my mind, was like a delicious poison I couldn't get enough of?

"I think we're go—" his words died and slowly, he turned his face until his eyes met mine. Oh, lord, if I stretched my neck, if I lifted on my tiptoes, my lips would touch his, and right now, that was all I could think about.

Killian's eyes darkened and his gaze flicked once to my mouth. So that was also on his mind. Then why didn't he surrender to it? We were here, alone in a goddamned tree, cocooned in each other. A boldness I didn't know I had invaded my pores and I reached for him.

The world swirled around me.

One moment, we were in the tree, the other, we stood beside the car, Killian several steps away from me.

He cleared his throat. "We should leave before more familiars show up." He slipped inside the car.

Tears brimmed in my eyes at the sting of rejection. Holy shit, why did I have to be such a fool?

I quickly wiped at my eyes, inhaled deeply to compose myself, and joined him in the car. "Turn around. Let's go back into town."

He didn't look at me as he put the car into drive and rounded the narrow road. "You've got a plan?"

"We'll see."

Thirty minutes later, Killian and I arrived at an inn outside of a small town. Killian found a spot in the parking lot and I immediately shoved open the car door, stepping out. Being stuck with Killian in a tight space was almost as smothering as my claustrophobia.

Leaning my ass on the car's side, I filled my lungs with the crisp air—cooling and energizing. Just what I needed.

My party was over when Killian decided to join me, though he kept his distance, and leaned against the car's hood.

"Can you hear them?" I asked, my eyes on the inn. It was outdated and clearly old, though it had a new coat of gray paint with black trim and doors.

"No," was all he said.

A car engine revved and I turned to the sound. A red sedan rolled in the parking lot. Asher was behind the wheel, and Evelyn beside him. Asher parked his car beside ours, and both of them stepped out.

"I didn't expect to see you here," Evelyn said as she walked closer.

"I think I found the witches you're looking for," I told her.

Eyes wide, Evelyn and Asher exchanged a look. "How do you know it's them?"

"Well, I don't, but they are hiding." I paused. "They were wearing ball gowns and they have familiars, like the witches at the Light Castle."

"That sounds like them," Asher said.

Killian shifted his weight. "It turns out, they might have something we're looking for too."

"So you want to join forces?" Evelyn asked, sounding a little too excited.

I nodded. "If the offer is still open."

One corner of Evelyn's lips quirked up. "Sure it is."

"What's your plan?" Killian went directly to the point.

"First, we need to scout the place, then we come up with a plan," Asher said.

I patted the car's door beside me. "Then let's go."

* * *

KILLIAN DROVE us in our car to the ski lodge. Evelyn and Asher took the backseat, but they had insisted on loading our trunk with their gear—potions, swords, and more—just in case.

As we took the narrow, winding road up the mountain, I shook my head, marveling at what my life had become. I had always known I was a witch, but it was still amusing, and unsettling, that now I fought against demons and evil witches, and ran from mad warlocks. Magic and supernaturals were now as common as breathing air and drinking water.

So was killing.

I shuddered.

This time, Killian stopped the car farther from the lodge, afraid the familiars would be out and about again.

"A ski lodge?" Asher asked. He and Evelyn leaned between the front seats, looking at the lodge.

"An abandoned one," Evelyn said. "I mean, it could be worse. Remember those witches who lived in a cave? Those were nasty."

Asher snickered. "We dubbed them cavitch."

Evelyn chuckled with him. "What will call these ones? Skiwitch? No. How about skitch?"

"Or lodgitch," Asher said, still laughing.

A hand squeezed my heart. They were so cute together; jealousy wormed through me.

Killian snarled, clearly annoyed.

I died a little more on the inside.

"We should get closer." I opened the car door, but a hand closed around my wrist.

"We shouldn't," Killian said. "The familiars could be anywhere. If we're discovered now, it's game over."

My lips pressed together, silencing the argument on the tip of my tongue and my temper with it; I wouldn't make a scene in front of Evelyn and Asher.

"I can go." Evelyn palmed a vial from her utility belt. "This will make me invisible for a few minutes."

She drank the amber liquid and left the car. Asher didn't say a word. He just sat back, his arms crossed over his chest and a proud smile on his lips.

Damn, where did Evelyn find one of those? I would have to talk to her.

Also ... "I'll have to talk to her about the potions. They're incredible."

"Evelyn doesn't like to rely on her magic, since dragon bones contain dark magic," Asher said.

Evelyn's body shimmered for a few seconds and then disappeared. So freaking cool.

"So she created potions."

My magic wasn't dark (I hoped), but it had been blocked from me. Thus why I played with potions. But Evelyn was on another level. I wished that we could spend time with them so she could teach me, but there was no time for that, unfortunately.

"It must come in handy for all sorts of things," I said.

"It does," Asher said. "Once, we were at a restaurant, quietly having dinner in a corner booth, when a kid had an allergic reaction to the nuts. It was the first time; his parents were shocked. While someone called 911, the kid was visibly dying. Evelyn spread the herbs on his back and guided the nuts out. He threw them up."

"That's amazing."

"Yeah, but a crowd of people saw her." He sighed. "We hopped on the road without finishing our dinner."

I frowned. I sometimes wondered how the world would be if supernaturals were outed to humans. From what Delia had told me, humans outnumbered supernaturals a hundred thousand to one. Even with all of our powers, we couldn't defeat them or keep them at bay if they decided we were a threat.

"Humans have a narrow view, don't they?" I asked, lost in thought.

"Most of the time, yes," Asher agreed. "I've yet to meet a human who completely accepted us as we are."

Though Asher wasn't a warlock, he still carried the witches' magical genes. He knew the witches' way and he could fight. He would be considered a supernatural like us.

Silence stretched in the car.

I glanced at my phone. Evelyn had been gone for almost thirty minutes. "How long will you give her?"

"An hour," Asher said, not sounding one bit worried.

"She's coming back now," Killian said. He must be hearing her heartbeat and maybe her footsteps. "And she's in a hurry."

One of the back doors opened and closed. Evelyn's body shimmered into existence again. "Go. Drive. You have to go."

Killian frowned, but didn't ask questions. He put the car into drive, turned around, and sped down the narrow road.

"What happened?" Asher asked, still not sounding worried.

"Two of them got into a Hummer and are coming this way." She leaned between the front seats and pointed to the road's shoulder, where there was a thick line of trees. "There. Drive behind those trees and hide. When they drive by, we follow."

Killian turned the car around and backed it behind the trees. From the lodge side, no one would be able to see it, not even witches.

Twenty seconds later, a black Hummer drove by.

"Go," I said at the same time Evelyn yelled, "Now!"

Killian snarled. "I'm going."

Killian maintained a good distance from the Hummer, and I thought we would lose it, but opened his window halfway down, listening for our quarry. The Hummer turned away from the little town we had been before, and twenty minutes later, arrived at another small town.

The Hummer stopped in front of a black building that reminded me of a giant shoebox. Two women dressed in elegant pencil skirts and jackets and high heels stepped out, one in black, the other in gray.

Killian parked our car a block away, in front of a pet store, blending in with the vehicles already parked on the street.

The witch in black knocked on the building's metal doors. A man with a round belly opened it. He took one look at them and stepped back, letting them in.

"Damn it," Killian muttered. "I can't hear them."

We waited. Ten minutes later, the witches emerged. They entered their car and left. Killian waited another minute for good measure, then moved our car to where the witches' Hummer had been parked.

The four of us got out of the car, but only Killian went to the door.

He knocked and the metal vibrated. A moment later, the same man opened the door. He narrowed his dark eyes at Killian, then glanced at us.

"What do you want?" he asked, his voice rough.

Killian stood right in front of the man. "Tell me what the witches wanted."

"To make sure everything is organized for their party tomorrow night," the man said, a robotic tone to his voice.

"What is this place?"

"A private clubhouse."

"And the witches have a party here tomorrow."

"Yes, but the club will be open for everyone. Their party will be upstairs, in the VIP section."

Killian turned to us. "Any more questions?" I couldn't

think of any. Evelyn and Asher shook their heads. Killian faced the man again. "Forget about us and this conversation." He pushed the man inside the door and closed it. Putting his hands inside the pockets of his jacket, Killian walked back to us. "You heard him. The witches have a party here tomorrow night."

"So, what's the plan?" I asked, wondering how we could work with this.

Evelyn looked me up and down. "Do you have a party dress?"

7

I DIDN'T HAVE A DRESS. NEITHER DID EVELYN. THANKFULLY, we found a store nearby and promptly bought two dresses we thought were appropriate for a night out.

The dress lay on my bed.

I stared at it, as if it were an alien.

I had never worn anything like this—tight, short, and revealing—and now that it was time for me to put it on, I felt sick to my stomach.

I was about to crash a dark witches' party.

There was also the vampire pacing between the two queen beds in this tiny hotel room. Since Evelyn came up with the idea of us going to the party, Killian had fallen into an even worse mood than before. He wasn't quiet and stoic anymore. He was brooding and annoyed.

It was getting on my last nerve.

I put my hands on my waist. "You're going to make a hole on the floor and fall into someone else's bedroom. Please stop."

"I can't." Killian clenched and unclenched his fingers

repeatedly. I noticed he had started with that a couple of days ago, and it was now more frequent.

Last evening, after hashing out our plan, we got a room at the same inn as Evelyn and Asher. But Killian barely spent the night here with me. Instead, he went out to feed and to think. Today, it wasn't much different. I had breakfast and lunch with Evelyn and Asher, and barely saw Killian the entire day. And every time I saw him, he looked madder.

"Please, just ... stop and talk to me. What's the matter?"

He did stop, but he stared at me as if I was dumb. "What's the matter? You're walking into the witches' web willingly."

"We've talked about this. It's the only way for us to get into the lodge. Or you would rather the four of us storm the ski lodge and try to take on countless witches?"

Killian ran a hand through his hair, messing the longer strands. "Are you really okay with this?"

He knew I wasn't okay. He could probably hear my rapid heartbeat and breathing, but I answered him anyway. "No, but what other choice do we have?"

Evelyn was so badass and sure of herself. When she proposed the plan with a confident gleam in her eyes, I couldn't deny her. Besides, the witches had a box and I couldn't leave it with them. I had to steal it before they figured out how to use it.

"I don't like this," he muttered.

That was his new favorite phrase.

I picked up the dress from the bed and went to the bathroom to take a quick shower, put on some makeup, and change. I had never been big on makeup and the only thing I wore were mascara and lip gloss, so yesterday after buying the dress, Evelyn and I stopped by a drugstore to buy cosmetics.

Now, in my underwear in front of the mirror, I applied foundation, eyeliner, mascara, blush, and red lipstick. I blinked at my reflection in the mirror. It wasn't bad at all, but it wasn't me. I finished it up by French braiding the sides of my wild dark hair and leaving the rest loose down my back. I picked up the ends and glanced at them—the red dye was fading. I would have to dye it again soon if I wanted to keep them.

At the drugstore, Evelyn had checked out perfumes, but ended up not picking any.

"I make my own perfume," she had said.

That had given me an idea.

I dug inside my herb bag and grabbed the vial with my signature oil. I poured a couple of drops in my palm, mixed with lavender powder, and then smeared that on my neck, my collarbone, and my wrists. It shouldn't be too strong, just enough to enhance my natural scent along with some sweet wafts from lavender.

Then, I put on the dress—an off-the-shoulders black tube that hugged my body like glue. It went down to the middle of my thighs, but I felt exposed. The dress had a delicate invisible zipper up the back, and when I pulled it, it got stuck at my waist.

Shit.

I glanced at the closed door. Knowing Killian, he had probably left the moment I stepped into the bathroom. Still, I cracked the door and spied out. To my surprise, he was seated on the edge of his bed.

He looked up at me and his eyes widened.

I stepped out of the bathroom. "Hm, I need help with the zipper."

As slowly as I had ever seen him move, Killian stood from

the bed. Holding my gaze, he walked toward me. I turned around and pulled my hair over my shoulder to give him better access to my back.

The first thing I felt was him. His body looming over me, his presence and power a tangible force against me. Then, his cold fingertips touched my lower back as he got ahold of the zipper and I inhaled deeply, suppressing a shiver that crawled up my spine. He tugged the zipper up, his fingers leaving a chilly trail across my skin. When he finished, he didn't pull his hands away; he didn't move back. Instead, he leaned over me, his nose an inch from my exposed neck. My knees grew weak as he inhaled deeply.

My mind warred with thoughts that finally, I had gotten him, or no, he was doing this because he wanted my blood, nothing else.

I glanced over my shoulder at him.

His green eyes were dark on mine, a seductive and dangerous glint in them.

"Thank you," I whispered.

He didn't move.

I braced myself and spun in place. Killian's hands moved from my back to my waist, but he didn't pull them back, and his entire body still loomed over me, his head one inch from mine.

"I don't want you to go," he said, his voice low and rough.

"I have to."

"But if you're in there, among dozens, maybe hundreds of witches, it'll be nearly impossible for me to help you."

Braver than I had felt in so long, I placed a hand on his chest. "I appreciate the sentiment, but I can do this."

His eyes searched mine. "Lavinia, I—"

A knock came from the door.

Killian snapped his head toward the sound and snarled.

I stilled. "What is it?"

"It's Evelyn and Asher," he replied. "They're ready."

I let out a breath and turned to the door. "Can you please open the door while I put on my shoes?"

Killian eyed me as I sat down on my bed and worked the laces of my black stilettos. Another knock came and he finally moved. He threw the door open, stepped back, and crossed his arms.

Ignoring the brooding vampire, Evelyn walked in. "Let me see."

I finished tying the last of the lace that came to the middle of my calf and stood. The urge to get a big jacket and hide was immense, but I raised my chin, straightened my spine, and lifted my arms to give her full view of the ensemble. "So?"

She wolf-whistle. "Girl, you look hot!"

My cheeks flamed. "Thanks. You too."

Evelyn had bought a burgundy one-shoulder dress that cinched at her waist and had an asymmetrical hemline. Her hair had been woven into an intricate ponytail and her long, black hair swished down her back. Two silver hoops and a small black purse completed the look.

Asher didn't look bad either. He wore dark gray slacks and a white shirt with a black swirling pattern. Two jackets were folded over his arm.

The only one still wearing street clothes was Killian.

"Ready?" Asher asked. He handed a jacket to Evelyn.

I nodded, grabbed my leather jacket from the bed, and headed for the door. We exited the room—except for Killian. I glanced back at him.

He fixed his gaze on me. "I'll meet you there."

My stomach dropped. "You're not coming?" I knew he didn't like our plan, and the fact that we were dealing with witches, but I hadn't expected him to bail on us.

On me.

Asher stepped closer. "But we need you to get us in."

"I'll meet you there," Killian repeated, a rumble in his throat.

He closed the room's door in my face. I stared at the crooked number on the door, confused. What the hell was going on with him?

"Come on, Lavinia," Evelyn called me, her voice soft. "We should go."

With one last glance at the closed door, I followed Asher and Evelyn to their car.

EVELYN SLID the car into a spot two blocks from the club.

Fifteen minutes ticked by, then the next fifteen.

Nervous energy rippled through me.

Asher turned around in the passenger seat, looking at me in the back. "Is he always this moody?"

Evelyn nudged him with her elbow.

"What? It's true. Even when he was helping with the bodies yesterday, he barely talked to me."

I sighed. "To be honest, I haven't known him long, but he has been moodier than usual, yes." I frowned, wondering how much I should disclose. "He has a thing against witches."

Evelyn raised her eyebrows. "But what about you?"

"I think he forgets what I am when it's just us, but now

that you're in the picture, and we're about to face more witches ... it has him on edge."

"I see," Evelyn whispered, facing the front again.

We watched as a few cars drove by and parked around ours. People wearing all kinds of clothes—formal dresses, jeans, sweaters—exited the cars and went to the club. Some got in, most didn't.

I glanced at my phone again. Another fifteen minutes went by. I could call Killian and ask him what was taking so long, or ...

"We're wasting time," I said. "We should try to get in without him." I opened the passenger door and hopped out of the car.

Killian walked toward us.

My breath caught.

Killian had changed into black slacks and dark purple shirt—with the sleeves folded to his elbows and two buttons undone at the collar. A gentle but chilly breeze ruffled the top of his hair, and he absently reached up and fixed it.

Holy shit, he was like a model on the catwalk.

My heart squeezed.

He stopped in front of me. "I'm sorry I'm late."

My brows dipped down. I needed to talk to him about what was going on, but now was not the time.

"Better late than never," Evelyn said. "Let's go."

She and Asher took the lead, walking fast toward the club.

Killian didn't move. His eyes fixed on mine. "I forgot to say before, but you look ... incredible."

Heat spread through my cheeks. "Thanks."

He offered me his arm and I took it—and I was glad, because on the way to the club, I tripped three times in the damned heels, and if Killian hadn't been an anchor, I would have kissed the concrete.

We caught up to Evelyn and Asher, and paused at the front of the short line. Killian knocked on the metal door, and the same man from yesterday opened it.

"Not—" He looked at Killian and froze.

"You'll let my friends and me in," Killian said.

The man opened the door and let us pass.

"Way too easy," Asher muttered as we stepped into a dark front room.

The darkness pressed against me and I inhaled sharply. Killian's hand rested over mine in the crook of his arm. He leaned into me, and in the dark, placed a kiss on the top of my head. "You're okay," he whispered in my ear. "I'm here with you."

My heart skipped a beat before speeding up.

A door opened on the other side of the room and a pink light streamed in.

"Having a vampire nearby can be very handy," Evelyn said, walking toward the door.

"What's the fun in that?" Asher asked. "We could have found a way of sneaking in. We always do."

Forgetting the darkness and Killian's tender moment, I focused on the couple in front of us. They were too cute together.

As we entered the back room, pink and blue lights blasted us, and the pounding beat of electronic music threatened to explode my skull. Scents of perfume and alcohol mixed in the air.

As we snaked through the crowd, I took in the place. A lobby opened to different areas of the club: a long mirrored bar lined the left wall, and metal, bar-height tables and stools lined the right. A polished dance floor occupied the space between the bar and seating. Past the dance floor were two men guarding wide metal stairs that led to the second floor. Balconies with glass railing jutted out from the second-story walls—the VIP area. The club wasn't large, but it was packed.

We made our way to the back through the side, avoiding the bodies bumping and humping on the dance floor. Killian walked behind me, a sure hand on my lower back.

Once we arrived in front of the two men, Killian stepped forward. He said something to the men. We couldn't hear him over the loud music, but the men immediately stepped aside to let us pass.

Evelyn looked at me. "Ready?"

I nodded.

She placed a quick kiss on Asher's lips and started climbing the stairs.

I took a step to follow her, but a hand shot out and closed around my wrist. I turned back and looked at Killian.

His brows curled down; he leaned into me. His breath teased my cheek before his mouth hovered over my ear. "Be careful," he whispered.

8

———

My palms sweated and my heart pumped against my rib cage. Holy shit, what was I doing? I had just met Evelyn and I was walking into a den of dark witches. Powerful ones who had probably been practicing magic their entire lives. Who was I to go against them? To outsmart them? This was crazy ...

But before I could rethink this, Evelyn halted in front of the largest archway on the second floor. Beyond it, at least two dozen women in cocktail dresses occupied the place, some of them standing close to the railing, some by the bar in the back, but most were seated on the black velvet couches, with drinks and food strategically placed on the mirrored tables. A handful of men clad in only black pants danced among them.

One of the women threw money at the men and the others laughed.

So this was how witches partied? Interesting ...

A witch rose from the couch, her eyes on us. She didn't lose her smile as she approached us, and goose bumps ran up my arms. She stepped out of the VIP room, forcing us to take a step back, and regarded us with her dark eyes.

Her narrow chin jutted out from under her blond, asymmetrical bob. "Who are you?" she asked, her voice impassive.

"I'm Evelyn," Evelyn said. "And this is my friend, Lavinia. We're witches and we would like to talk to you."

The witch narrowed her eyes at us and took mine and Evelyn's hands. I swallowed hard, and fighting the urge to spy on Evelyn, I slipped my hand in hers. She gripped my hand tight and closed her eyes, inhaling deeply.

I braced for magic to invade me, to prod and search, to envelop me, but there was nothing. No magic, no sensation, not even a tickle.

"Hm." The witch opened her eyes and dropped our hands. "All right. Follow me." She went back to the velvet couches and shooed some of the other witches, making space for us beside her.

Evelyn and I exchanged a glance and then walked into the VIP area. We sat one on each side of the witch. Instantly, two men knelt in front of us with silver trays full of drinks. The witch grabbed a flute of silver liquid. Evelyn picked a red one, and I grabbed a pink drink.

"I'm Cyrene," she said. Here the music wasn't so loud and it was easier to hear. "So, how did you hear about us?"

"We heard rumors that a witch coven lived nearby and we came looking for you," Evelyn said. We had rehearsed this before.

Cyrene drank from her glass. "Why?"

"We've been on our own for a long time," I said. "We've been hunted by light witches and the Brotherhood. We're tired of fighting them alone."

Cyrene looked at us. "You want to join our coven?"

"Is that a possibility?" Evelyn asked.

"It depends." Cyrene leaned back and downed the rest of her drink. "Hang around. Have fun. We can talk more about this later."

She stood up and sashayed out of sight.

Evelyn turned to me. "She didn't introduce herself as the queen or princess of the coven," she whispered.

Earlier today, when we were getting ready for tonight, Evelyn explained to me a few things I should know about witch covens. Most of them had a queen at the helm, or a princess, if the queen was unavailable—or had died recently. There were several kinds of witches. Their powers presented in different ways, and they lived by different rules. However, light and dark witches had a queen or princess and a council to help them rule. And the freakiest info of all: the covens kept the heart of the first witch of their coven, a powerful relic that was thousands of years old, but kept the magic in their bloodlines alive.

Evelyn also told me that once upon a time, the light and dark witches weren't divided. They lived as one big coven, the Lightmist coven. But about seven hundred years ago, Arianna, the most powerful witch ever alive, was worried about the witch hunts and separated the magics. She founded the Lightgrove coven, for only light witches. The dark witches formed the Darkmist coven.

Time passed, the covens grew. The Lightgrove became selective, only accepting witches of great power into their ranks. As far as Evelyn knew, Darkmist wasn't as selective, though it didn't accept just anyone into its midst either. Other smaller and less powerful covens started popping up everywhere. And this coven was one of them—the Nightmist coven.

"But she seems like a high-ranked witch," I said. "Maybe she's part of the council."

Evelyn nodded. "Probably."

Two witches scooted closer to us.

"Hi there," a red-haired one said, wearing a naughty smile. "I'm Lorie."

"And I'm Keeva," the blonde said, holding a thin, long pipe. I recognized them from yesterday—they were the ones on the balcony. Their hairdos were different, and they wore normal party dresses, not puffy gowns, but I was sure it was them.

We introduced ourselves, and when they asked why we were here, we offered them the same answer we had given Cyrene.

"We're glad you're here," Lorie said.

Keeva nodded. "Yeah, we love new witches." She picked up a silver plate from the mirrored table to her left and offered the finger foods to us. "Try a few. This one is my favorites."

I didn't want to give them any reason to kick us out of there, so I grabbed a little puff topped with shrimp, and Evelyn picked up a chip with colorful nuts. I shoved it in my mouth, and to my surprise, it wasn't shrimp. I had no idea what it was, but it tasted sweet and sugary.

"It's good," Evelyn said, after swallowing.

"I know, right?" Lorie said. She took a drag from her pipe.

"So, what's the occasion?" I asked, genuinely curious.

"Oh, it's Dot's birthday." Keeva pointed to a tall witch with smooth olive skin and black curls. She wore a long golden dress, and for a moment, I was sure she was a goddess, not a witch. "She's turning one hundred!"

I almost choked. "What?" She didn't look a day over

twenty-five. I mean, I knew witches aged slower than humans, but even Delia had had a few lines around her eyes at forty.

"She's one of our oldest," Lorie said. "Her grandmother lived to be three hundred and twenty-seven. She'll probably live just as long."

"Or longer," Keeva added.

Lorie nodded.

The song changed to a slower, sensual ballad. The human men in the center of the room started dancing closer, moving their hips in suggestive ways. A couple of them took off their pants, wearing only their tight boxers.

Oh my God …

Embarrassed, I averted my eyes, but I couldn't deny the pull it had on me. On everyone. All witches, including Evelyn, peeked at them, their eyes shining with interest, some with desire. Evelyn widened her eyes at me. I sent her a mental message that I knew she wouldn't hear: *I know!* The humans were handsome and probably spent a lot of time working out—the witches knew how to pick them—but for some reason, I didn't feel like I should stare at them like the others did.

Why was I lying to myself? I wasn't looking and admiring the hot men because I was interested in a certain vampire who was currently downstairs. Drooling at these men felt like … I don't know, cheating?

I let out a long sigh.

Cheating was for people in relationships. At the moment, I didn't even know if Killian and I were partners anymore—*business* partners.

"I can't just watch," Lorie said. She stood up, grabbed one of the men by the wrist, and dragged him to a dark corner.

My eyes widened as she pressed him to the wall and kissed him.

Keeva laughed. "Way to go, Lor!" She jumped to her feet and joined the men in the center, dancing among them—and rubbing her hands over their hard torsos, and slapping their asses.

Oh my ...

Evelyn leaned closer to me. "They sure do like their men."

"I know," I whispered. I looked around. All the witches were engaged in something. Keeva and another were dancing with the humans; some stood to the side, talking, laughing, and drinking; some sat on the couches by our side, playing some kind of board game; and Lorie was in the corner, her skirt hiked to her thighs and moving in a way—

Holy shit, she was having sex with the guy! In front of everyone.

I snapped my head back, mortified.

"Cyrene is at the bar," Evelyn said. "She has two witches with her, but she's not interacting with them. She's watching us."

"Shit." She was evaluating us. "We can't give her a reason to send us away."

"Agreed. We should mingle with the witches, do what they are doing."

My brow furrowed. "I will not dance with these men."

Evelyn rolled her eyes. "Me neither, but we need to do *something*." She grabbed my hand and stood, taking me with her.

She squeezed us among the men and I had to bite the inside of my cheek so I wouldn't squirm out of the way. Keeva saw us and cheered with her arms up. She stepped to our side and danced with us. She pulled Dot to our small circle in a circle and introduced us to the birthday witch.

Three other witches joined us and suddenly it wasn't so awkward, especially when I could stay away from the men dancing around us. For a moment, I even forgot what we were doing there. That these were dark witches, and we had come to infiltrate their ranks. For a moment, I was a twenty-year-old woman on a girls' night out with her friends.

But these weren't my friends. I couldn't even say that of Evelyn, not yet.

A somber feeling fell over my shoulders.

A waiter strolled past us, shaking his hips to the beat of the song. I stepped out of the circle, grabbed what looked like a wine goblet, and halted beside the glass railing.

I needed a minute to myself.

I took a sip from my glass—yes, it was wine—and looked down at the humans dancing in the club, clueless of the creatures lurking around. But I wasn't interested in them. No, the one I was interested in was easy to find. He stuck out from the others as if he was silk in the midst of rolls of burlap. Killian stood beside a tall table, his hip leaned against it, and his eyes directly on me.

My heart squeezed and heat traveled lower in my stomach. After the almost naked men, the sensual dancing, and Lorie and the human having sex in front of everyone, my body felt hot and in need.

And there was only one person I wanted to put out the fire.

One who had distanced himself from me. One who ultimately hated my kind. One who had partnered with me because of the damn box, nothing more.

It's just his power, I told myself. *Just his vampire magic.*

I kept forgetting that allure was part of a vampire's power. That was why I felt like running down the stairs, pushing him into a dark corner, and doing to him what Lorie was doing to that human. Right?

Right?

I wasn't so sure anymore.

I held his stare, trying to decipher him, even though we were so far apart, in this loud and dark place, and—

"Are you enjoying your night?"

I turned to face Cyrene. She halted by my side at the railing, a green drink in her hand, and I prayed to the spirits she hadn't figured out who I was staring at. I plastered a soft smile on my lips. "Very much. It's much better than running, hiding, and running again." I had to pitch our case, as if Evelyn and I were two poor orphans who desperately needed a new home.

"How did you and Evelyn meet?"

We had rehearsed this too. "A couple of years ago. The Brotherhood of Purity had rounded us up along with a handful of other witches. They were going to execute us but Evelyn and I escaped." My face fell.

Evelyn joined us.

Cyrene looked from her to me. "What do the two of you have to offer the Nightmist coven?"

"Our magic, wit, and determination," Evelyn said. "There's strength in numbers. Two more witches might be what makes Nightmist more powerful."

Cyrene narrowed her eyes at us. "Usually, we invite witches to our coven, and even that is rare. But you two showed initiative and grit by coming to us. Since it's not normal for us to let outsiders join us, we will require you to pass a test."

I was waiting for that; Evelyn had told me it was common when joining light or dark witches' covens ...

"A test?" Evelyn feigned ignorance.

Cyrene nodded. "You have to prove your worth, if you're fit to join the coven." She picked up my wrist, turn my hand so my palm was up, and drew an X with her fingers on my skin. "Be at this location at six in the evening. If you're one second late, you automatically fail the test." She lifted her glass at us. "Enjoy the rest of the party."

9

"Here," Evelyn reached across the two front seats and handed me a small vial with a black liquid.

I took it. "This is it?"

"Yup. It'll give you fake powers for an hour or two," she explained.

I glanced from the vial to Killian, seated behind the steering wheel. He had been even quieter and more impassive since we came back to the inn from the club late last night.

For appearances, Evelyn and I stayed at the club for another three hours, until the party started to wind down. We told Cyrene we had been traveling and looking for them for weeks and were tired, and she didn't seem one bit concerned about it.

Killian and Asher waited for us at the car, parked a good ways from the club. Asher kissed Evelyn on the lips and asked dozens of questions of how it had been, what we talked about, what they said, and more. Killian, on the other hand, barely looked at me as we all hopped in the car and drove back to the inn.

When we were all inside Evelyn's and Asher's bedroom, I opened my hand and showed them the invisible X on my palm. A dark light glowed from it and an image appeared over it, hovering in the air like a hologram—a stone archway in front of a stone path flanked by tombstones.

A cemetery, of course.

After that, Killian and I headed to our bedroom, but he didn't come in. He told me he wanted to go feed, but would be back. Disappointed once more, I entered the room by myself, took a shower to take the scent of the club and the sweat off my skin, and plopped in bed.

I slept until noon the next day, and in the afternoon, the four of us got together to talk about the test. We had no idea what it would be, how long it would be, but one thing was certain: the guys couldn't be nearby, and the witches would test our magic. Meaning: I was screwed. And because of that, Evelyn spent the rest of the afternoon working on potions— and I helped.

Now we were in our car, parked on the back road leading to the cemetery, a good three blocks away. In about fifteen minutes, the guys would stay in the car, while Evelyn and I walked to the cemetery.

"Here goes nothing," I muttered before downing the vial. I gagged, the thick and sour liquid catching in my throat.

"Sorry." Evelyn wrinkled her nose. "I probably should have told you what to expect."

I shook my head. "No, it's good that you didn't. If I had known, I would have drunk it slowly and it would have been worse." Despite the taste, I could feel it working. A warmth filled my veins, fueling my magic. Hopefully, this would be enough.

Evelyn looked at Asher, Killian, and then me. She raised her eyebrows at me. "I ... I'll stretch my legs outside before we go." She opened her door and pulled Asher to get out of the car with her.

Outside, Evelyn and Asher talked while she stretched. A soft smile adorned my lips. She didn't need to do that. Everyone knew she had said that to give Killian and me some space.

Then, my eyebrows slammed down and I turned to Killian. "Look, I can only imagine what's going on here, but I'm tired of your coldness and bullshit. If you're so bothered by being around me, around Evelyn, then leave. Take your box and go to DuMoir Castle."

Killian's eyes darkened. "What about you?"

I showed him my cell phone. "I'll call you once I have the other box. You can tell me exactly where you are and I'll come to you. I'll hand you the second box ..." And then what? Shouldn't I stay there too to figure out my connection to the boxes? No, what came after didn't matter. Right now, I had to focus on what we could do in the present moment.

"And what about the warlocks?"

Shit. Since bumping into Evelyn and Asher and sensing the second box, I hadn't even thought about the warlocks.

"I'll be with Evelyn and Asher," I told him. "And if it comes to that, I'll use the power in the second box to defend myself."

"I don't like this," he muttered.

Here we go again.

"Then leave!" God, he would drive me crazy.

Killian stared at me, his gaze so intense, it made me breathless. "I can't, Lavinia. Don't you get that? I can't walk away from you."

I gaped at him. "What the hell does that mean?"

He inhaled deeply and turned his body toward me a little more. "I—"

A knock on the window made me jump. My heart raced triple time. "Holy shit," I whispered.

Evelyn pointed to her phone and mouthed, "Time to go."

Shaking my head, I opened the door.

"Lavinia—"

I whipped around in the passenger seat and glared at Killian. "No, don't. I'm tired of your attitude." I gestured to the entirety of him. "You need to figure it out ... then, you talk to me about it. Until then, stick to business."

I exited the car, straightened my leather jacket, and filled my lungs with the cold evening air. It was really cold at night this time of the year, but I had no idea what the test would entail. If it involved something physical, I wanted to be able to move, thus the leggings, the thermal tee, and the leather jacket. My boots, and the dagger inside one of them, completed my let's-woo-these-witches look.

Evelyn was dressed in a similar fashion, though instead of leggings, she wore skinny jeans, and a thin jean jacket with wool lining. She had pulled her long hair in a ponytail, and had her utility belt overflowing with potions and powders. She had given me a couple of her special brews earlier, and those now were safely stored inside my pockets.

I picked up my bag from the trunk and put it inside Asher's and Evelyn's car. They had come in their car, because if we passed the test, it was probable that Evelyn and I would have to have our own mode of transportation out of here. When we had arrived here, they had gotten into our car so we could talk about our loose plan and to hand out potions.

I checked the time on my phone. "We better go."

She turned to Asher and I looked away as they said goodbye to each other, and hugged and kissed. I heard Asher whispering, "Good luck, Evie. I love you."

Jealousy's ugly claws shredded deep holes in my chest.

When Evelyn showed up at my side, ready, we marched toward the cemetery. The first few yards, we walked in silence. Then, when we were a safe distance, even from vampire's ears, she said, "I'm sorry he's been giving you a hard time."

I scoffed. "Not as much as I am."

"Is there anything I can do?"

"I don't think so." I didn't think there was anything anyone could. "Thanks, though."

She offered me a small smile. "Anytime."

We then reached the cemetery and its metal archway entrance, I hesitated—the place was dark, with only a couple of working lampposts spread out through the large expanse of darkness.

I slipped my hand inside my pocket and felt my magical flashlight in there. I didn't want to use it in front of Evelyn, but it was comforting to know I had it, just in case.

Evelyn looked at me but didn't say anything. I caught up with her and we crossed under the archway, following the stone path leading deeper into the cemetery. Tombstones lined the way, their facades cracked and worn by time, while a few had fresh flowers nestled at their bases. Mausoleums sprouted out of the black, gothic angel statues keeping watch over their gates.

The path forked into three paths before a large mausoleum with statues of hooded figures.

"What now?" I asked, looking at the three paths.

Evelyn turned in a circle. "I don't know."

"Now, we talk."

Evelyn and I turned to the voice. Cyrene, wearing a black gown, stepped out from the shadows of the mausoleum's door. A handful of other witches, including Lorie, Keeva, and Dot, rounded the building and approached us, all of them wearing formal dresses and updos.

A raven circled the sky above us before settling on the mausoleum's slanted roof.

A sliver of apprehension snaked up my spine. Scary and powerful magic radiated from these witches.

Evelyn opened her arms. "We are here and ready."

Cyrene glanced from her to me. "I'm pleased you came."

"Thank you for this opportunity," I said, hoping that some niceties would gain points in our favor.

"Yes, and what an opportunity it is." Cyrene advanced until she was right in front of us, in the square's center. "We don't do this often, so you should be grateful and you should do your best to impress us during your test."

I nodded.

"Will the test take place now?" Evelyn asked.

"Now and here," Cyrene said. "We just need to establish some rules first." One corner of her lips curled up. "You can't leave the cemetery, there's a time to accomplish the test, and you can use any magical resource you have, except for outside help. Otherwise, you instantly fail."

I stilled. Hm, did she know Killian and Asher were a couple of blocks from here, waiting to hear from us? I hoped not.

"All right," I muttered, trying to hide my nervousness.

"I'll tell you about the test," Cyrene continued. "And then you'll have one hour to finish it. Are you ready?"

Evelyn nodded and I rolled my shoulders.

"In the flowers and the bed, you'll find the key, use it to unlock the dead, the truth you will see, defeat the darkness and the weak, and you'll get what you seek."

"A riddle," Evelyn whispered.

Cyrene's smile widened. "Exactly. Solve it in an hour or less. I'll see you two later."

She waved her hand and a tornado of dark smoke surrounded us. As quickly as it came, the smoke was gone. Along with the witches. I glanced around the cemetery; Evelyn and I were alone.

"What was it again?" Evelyn asked.

I focused. "In the flowers and the bed, you'll find the key, use it to unlock the dead, the truth you will see, defeat the darkness and the weak, and you'll get what you seek."

"In the flowers and the bed," Evelyn repeated. "That sounds like a grave with flowers. We saw plenty of those before."

We retraced our steps to the stone path and stopped beside the first tombstone with fresh flowers we saw.

I glanced to a few others around us. "How do we know which one is the right one?"

Evelyn shrugged. "Maybe it's any of them? Help me look for the key." She knelt in front of the tombstone and started rummaging through the flowers.

I frowned. This didn't seem right. "Maybe—"

A piercing shriek filled the night and I stilled. "What the hell was that?"

Slowly, Evelyn stood up. "Shit, I think I know."

A white hand surged up from among the flowers. I swallowed a yelp and stepped back. "Is that a ghost?"

The hand lifted, revealing an arm, then a head of a woman with crazy floating hair, hollow eyes, and missing teeth.

Definitely a ghost.

"It's not the only one," Evelyn said. I followed her gaze, and true enough, at least a dozen ghosts surrounded us—all of them human in form, but milky in color, translucent, and floating off the ground.

I sucked in a sharp breath as my heart sped up. Shit, I had never seen a ghost before. "Will they hurt us?"

"It depends," she said. "I've dealt with ghosts before." She reached for something in her utility belt. "We just need—"

The ghosts let out another horrifying shriek and advanced toward us. I let out the yelp lodged in my throat, grabbed Evelyn's arm, and ran up the stone path again.

The ghosts were slower than us, but they kept coming. When the path forked, we picked the one on the right and kept going. We stopped behind a giant angel statue that loomed over two tombstones.

I frowned. "The riddle said, 'unlock the dead,' so we did, right?"

"It also said, 'you'll find the key,' and we sure didn't," Evelyn said, her breathing a little shallow from running. "Maybe these aren't the dead we're supposed to unlock." She picked up a small leather pouch from her belt. She turned it and red powder fell on her cupped hand. She handed the pouch and the rest of the powder to me. "Here. Throw some of the powder on them and say, '*Liberi*,' it should work."

I took the pouch. "You want us to face the damn ghosts?"

"I've done this quite a lot before." She spied from behind the statue. "Besides, the riddle said something about defeating the darkness and the weak. Maybe we have to free them. Then we'll be done."

Evelyn stepped back into the path and held her ground as the ghosts approached. She threw the powder on the nearest ghosts and said, "*Liberi*."

Two ghosts exploded into a million tiny sparks that disappeared in the air.

All right, we could do this.

I joined her and in less than a minute, we freed all the ghosts. I turned around, looking for more. "That was it?"

"It should be, right?"

"But what about the key part of the riddle?"

Evelyn pursed her lips. "Shit, there's that too."

Another shriek echoed through the air, raising the hairs on my arms. Sure enough, more ghosts rose from their graves.

My nose wrinkled as I watched them. "These are different. Look at their color." These ghosts weren't whitish, but darker, and their features seemed wrong—their mouths were large, their limbs elongated.

"I see it," Evelyn whispered. "I haven't seen these before."

Another shriek made me jump and the ghosts rushed to us—their mouths opened wide, revealing sharp teeth, and their hands became claws.

Evelyn held her ground and threw the powder at the closest one. The ghost shimmered, but remained. In fact, it turned darker and growled at us.

"Run!" I yelled.

Evelyn and I darted away, following the path deeper into the cemetery.

Thankfully, the ghosts weren't fast and we were able to get a reasonable distance from them. At another fork in the path, we found a big stone mausoleum with flowers swirls and engravings decorating the exterior.

"Let's hide in here," Evelyn said, pushing the heavy iron wrought doors open.

I froze. A dark and tiny mausoleum? That seemed like the perfect recipe for a claustrophobia attack, and that was the last thing I needed right now. My palms started sweating just thinking about it.

I shook my head. "I can't."

"Just come in here," Evelyn hissed.

I took a step back. No, I couldn't. I would rather face the damn ghosts than be trapped inside that place. I looked at the mausoleum, focusing on something else other than the darkness and the claustrophobia. The mausoleum was a beautiful rectangle with stone walls, wide metal windows, and a sharp inclined roof. Instead of being decorated with angels, it had delicate pots of plants in the corners, delicate flowers and leaves sprouting from them, and running up the walls. And it was all made of stone.

I frowned and took a better look at the wrought iron door and windows—the metal curved, forming vines and flowers.

In the flowers and the bed.

I gasped. "Evelyn, this is the place."

She poked her head out the door. "What are you talking about?"

"In the flowers and the bed." I pointed to all the flowers around the mausoleum.

"Oh, I see it now. Here's the bed." She gestured for me to follow her inside.

Shit. I couldn't step in, so I stopped outside the door. I fished my flashlight from my pocket and aimed it into the mausoleum's interior. Sure enough, there was a huge tomb in the center, the same pattern of stone flowers around it.

"The key must be in there."

"Come help me look," Evelyn said.

Shit. "I can't." I gritted my teeth. "I—"

"I found something!"

I aimed my flashlight at her, even though she couldn't see its light. Evelyn ran her fingertips along the stone vines covering the bottom of the tomb, and then over the flowers at their tips. She paused at the central flower.

"This one seems detached." She gently turned it and pulled it, revealing a smooth metal stick—like a key. Holding the key, she stood. "Wow, we found it."

"Now, we need to 'unlock the dead.'"

"But ... what does that mean?"

"What was the next verse? 'Use it to unlock the dead, the truth you will see.' And how do we unlock the dead?"

"Maybe there's another place to put this key?"

I glanced around the walls, looking for a keyhole. "It should be around here, right? I mean this is the bed and flowers thing."

"Right." Evelyn returned inside the tomb and I looked on the outside. This mausoleum was old and cracked, so it seemed there was a keyhole every three inches. I continued around the mausoleum, looking up and down, dusting away cobwebs and dust that could be covering the damn keyhole.

I took a step back and looked at the mausoleum. I probably should be close to see the tiny holes, but for some reason, I wanted to see the big picture.

I gasped as I took the back wall in—double doors were engraved on the stone between two metal windows, with stone flowers around it.

And there was a small hole right where the lock of the engraved door would be.

"Evelyn!" I called to her.

I heard her footsteps before I saw her rounding the mausoleum. She stumbled and looked back. "Shit, the ghosts are coming. We need to finish this now."

I pointed to the door. "Here."

"Oh, wow," she whispered. She fumbled with the key for a second, then placed it in the keyhole. Looking at me, she turned.

A click sounded loud and clear. A rumbling came from inside the mausoleum. Evelyn and I approached one of the windows and spied inside. The top of the tomb moved to the side and a corpse sat up.

I pressed a hand over my mouth before I screamed and brought the ghosts' and this skeleton's attention to us.

"What do we do now?" Evelyn asked, in a low voice, her eyes wide. She seemed as disturbed as I was.

"I don't know," I answered truthfully.

The skeleton crawled out the tomb, its bones cracking with each stiff move. I pointed my flashlight at it and took a good look—there was no flesh, just bones and sinew, and rags of clothes that once had probably been a nice pair of pants and shirt. The skeleton hobbled to the door and exited the mausoleum.

Careful, Evelyn and I tiptoed around the building and

spied out. The ghosts approached, all of them bloodthirsty with their teeth bared, their claws out.

The skeleton stomped a foot on the ground. "Quiet!" it screamed, a lot louder and a lot firmer than I thought possible.

Instantly, the ghosts dissipated into dust and nothing.

I exchanged a wide-eyed look with Evelyn. What the what?

The skeleton hobbled forward. "Who disturbs my sleep?"

What now? Did we hide here until the skeleton goes back to sleep?

"Remember the riddle," Evelyn whispered to me. "'Defeat the darkness and the weak'?"

The darkness ... what did that mean? I just hoped it wasn't literal.

"Ah-ha!" The skeleton jumped in front of us.

Evelyn and I scurried back, almost tripping over each other. My heart jumped to my throat.

"No need to hide, pretties," it said. Almost as fast as Killian, the skeleton ran around us, before stopping right in our faces. "I can find you anywhere."

On instinct, I kicked the skeleton in the stomach. It stumbled back. Evelyn grabbed my hand and we ran.

Past the mausoleum and into—

I stopped short.

Defeat the darkness and the weak.

"No, Evelyn, here," I said, pointing to the mausoleum. "I think ... we have to return the key."

She frowned. "I'm okay with anything at this point." Still holding my hand, she ran inside the mausoleum.

I went with her.

I braced myself for the panic. I felt it coming up my chest, but I focused on the light from my lantern, and the moonlight streaming through the windows. I could do this. I had to do this.

"What now?" Evelyn asked, looking around.

I had defeated the darkness by coming here. Now we had to defeat the weak, but how?

An idea sparked in my mind. I took the key from Evelyn as the skeleton hobbled into the mausoleum.

"There you are, my pretties," it said. "You came to spend some time at my home?" It cackled, and I almost dropped the key.

With trembling hands, I put the key back in its place and turned, until the flowers joined the others in the stone.

The skeleton stopped.

It fell to the ground, a heap of bones and rags.

I let out a long breath. "Holy shit, I thought it was going to drag us inside the tomb with it." Then, I would have the worst panic attack ever seen in modern history.

Evelyn pressed a hand to her chest, breathing hard. "Me too."

Claps sounded from the outside. Evelyn and I walked out and found Cyrene and the other witches standing right there.

"Congratulations," Cyrene said. The raven was perched on her shoulder. "You've passed the test."

Evelyn and I smiled at each other. Though it was nerve-racking, the test had also been exciting. It felt good to work alongside Evelyn.

"Thank you," I whispered, still shaken from all the running, the darkness, ghosts, and skeletons. I could use a break from all of it.

"Are you ready to go?" Cyrene asked. "Are your things nearby?"

"Yes, we left our things in our car," I said.

"Good. Then let's go meet the princess."

"The princess?" Evelyn asked. They hadn't mentioned her before.

One corner of Cyrene's lips tugged up. "Yes. She's very eager to meet you both."

10

EVELYN FOLLOWED THE WITCHES' HUMMER TO THE LODGE, AS if we didn't know where their coven was located. As we approached the ski lodge, the gates opened and the snow melted along a wide stone drive that led to the main door. But it didn't stop there. The path rounded to the side and disappeared into a garage door underneath the lodge, hidden by the mountainside. We went into the underground garage, parking beside the witches' Hummer.

Three black SUVs, two Jeeps, a red sports car, and two big sedans, plus a few snowmobiles and the Hummer, filled the garage.

These witches were obscenely wealthy.

Lorie, Keeva, Dot, and the other witches disappeared through a door to our left.

"This way." Cyrene gestured to the same door.

Despite the erratic way my heart beat in my chest, Evelyn and I didn't hesitate as we followed her into the lodge. The first thing we saw was wooden stairs, a long corridor with doorways, and a big room, which had probably been the lodge's main lobby. Though I had imagined a ski lodge full of wooden furniture and a gift shop near the front, and a check-in and information area on the other side. It didn't look anything like that now.

The wide stone fireplace and the floor-to-ceiling glass walls and windows were probably the only features from the original place. Now, dark rugs covered most of the wooden floors, sleek metal and leather chairs and lounges formed a wide semicircle around the fireplace, and where the front desk used to be was now a bar with colorful bottles and glasses of all sizes and shapes.

More witches were here, all dressed in ball gowns. Some lay on the loungers, others grabbed drinks from the bar. One changed the song on the jukebox in the corner, and another played with the fire, making it spark higher and higher.

Their conversation stopped as we entered the lobby, their eyes fixed on us. Lorie, Keeva, Dot, and the two others who had been with us dispersed and joined their sisters.

Cyrene gestured for us to follow her.

So we did.

We took a corridor on other side of the lobby. Doors lined the gray walls, former guest rooms that now served as the witches' suites. We turned a corner and came face-to-face with double doors. Two men dressed in dark leather and sporting sheathed swords at their waists stood on each side of the door.

The two men saw Cyrene and instantly opened the doors for her. She walked in.

Evelyn looked at me; I looked at her. We followed.

The events room with a tall ceiling and crystal chande-liers that refracted the artificial light. Like the lobby, an entire left wall was made of glass from floor to ceiling, with doors that opened to a balcony overlooking the slopes. To the right were a pool table, leather couches, a giant flat TV, and a fully equipped mini bar.

In the center of the room was a big leather armchair, flanked by two men in dark leather and swords. A woman wearing a black gown with a tight corset sat, nestled among its plush cushions. Her full breasts peeked from the top of her bodice, and I wondered if her waist was that tiny naturally. She had long, light-brown curls, dark-brown eyes, and smooth light-olive skin. As we approached her, her black lips stretched into a smile.

"Lavinia and Evelyn," she said, her voice thin, almost delicate. "It's so nice to meet you."

Cyrene stepped forward and bowed her head slightly. "Lavinia, Evelyn, this is Princess Fabula of the Nightmist coven."

Evelyn lowered her head like Cyrene had done and I rushed to do the same.

"I heard you passed our test," Princess Fabula said, sounding proud. "That's a great feat. Welcome to the Nightmist coven, my darling witches."

"Thank you," Evelyn and I said in unison.

"Cyrene here, my second in command, told me you two haven't been around witches that much growing up. That's a shame."

"We both lost our parents when we were younger," I said. To my surprise, my voice sounded normal, strong.

"That's such a shame." Princess Fabula's smile faded. "But now you found a new family. Since you're new to all of this, I'll tell you a bit about our coven." She stood but didn't move away from her chair. "A couple of centuries ago, a powerful witch called Brielle had a disagreement with the queen of the Darkmist coven and decided to leave. She knew there were several other smaller covens, but she didn't want to join a small coven. So, she created her own. The Nightmist coven. She was our first princess, and I'm her granddaughter."

I fought the urge to frown. Hm, why no queens? Why a princess?

"Princess Brielle, rest in darkness," Cyrene muttered from our right.

Creepy much?

"We grew by leaps and bounds, and we're now one of the biggest dark witch covens in North America." She opened her arms, proud of herself. "And as you can see,"—she pointed her open hands to the men standing by her sides—"we even have our own Dark Order."

Oh, so that was the Dark Order. The opposite of the Light Order with the Lightgrove witches, the one Asher's mother wanted to create.

"That's great," Evelyn said, her voice tight. Hopefully, Princess Fabula didn't know her voice well enough to tell. But I could see she was having a hard time with this.

"Isn't it?" Princess Fabula beamed. "All right. I know you're tired, so I'll let you go, but report to the main hall in two hours. We'll celebrate the newcomers." She winked at us, then sat back down in her chair.

Cyrene nodded her head to the door. Evelyn and I followed her out. The Dark Order men closed the door behind us.

"Don't get too excited," she said, walking down the hallway. "We always come up with any excuse to throw parties."

"Still, it's an honor," I said, and Evelyn nodded.

"Anyway, I'll give you a quick tour of the place, then show you to your bedrooms. Please, follow me."

Cyrene went around the lodge showing us room after room. Right beside the fake-throne room was another events' room, empty for now. She also showed us the kitchen and the main hall where a long wooden table and chairs took over the floor—where the party would be tonight. There was a music room, a game room, a movie room, a library, a sauna, an indoor pool, a hot tub in a sunroom, and much more. The lodge was bigger than it had looked from the outside, with several sides carved into the mountain.

We passed through a heavy wooden door with intricate metalwork and a huge lock.

Cyrene didn't say anything about it, but I couldn't help it. I stopped. "What is in here?"

"This door and beyond is off-limits," Cyrene said, her voice hard. "Only the coven's oldest members and the princess have access to this place. Understood?"

We nodded in acknowledgment, but once she turned her back to us and resumed her tour, I glanced at Evelyn. She lifted her eyebrows at me.

What could be beyond those doors?

The tour didn't take much longer and ended when Cyrene presented us to our new bedrooms on the third floor.

"There should be clean sheets and towels, and some clothes in the closets," she told us. "If you need anything, snap your fingers and whisper my name. Or Lorie's, or Keeva's. They will come to assist you."

"Thank you," I said, in front of my bedroom's door.

"I'll see you both in the main hall in a bit." Then she turned and left.

Once Cyrene turned a corner, Evelyn pushed me inside my bedroom. It wasn't as fancy as the hotel in New Orleans, but it was better than my bedroom back home. Large, with wooden floors, a king-sized bed with fluffy dark blue covers, an armchair and table in the corner, a tall dresser, a flat TV, mini fridge, and on the other side, a small closet and a bathroom—just like most hotel rooms.

Evelyn closed the door behind us and locked it. "That forbidden area ..."

"Yeah. I think the dragon bones and the box are there too." Along with whatever else these witches could be hiding.

"We need to sneak in there."

I frowned. "First, we need to get ready to attend this damn celebration tonight. We need to do what they tell us to, within reason, until we figure out if the items are in there, and how to sneak in there and get out undetected."

"I know." Evelyn started pacing. "I'm just ... impatient. And being here in the middle of these witches." She shuddered. "I don't like it."

I didn't like it either. Killian didn't like it. And even though I hadn't heard him saying it out loud, I was sure Asher also didn't like it. But it was the only way we could be here, right where we were now, and attack from the inside.

"If we do anything wrong, if we give them any reason to suspect us, they will kill us," I reminded her.

"I know, I know," she said with a sigh. "I promise I'm more levelheaded than this. Sorry, I'm just losing my head a little. I'll go to my bedroom, rest and get ready, and refocus. Tonight, we just pretend we're happy to be here."

I nodded. "Right."

"All right. I'll knock when I'm ready and we can go." Evelyn waved at me from the door before exiting and closing it.

Then I was alone in this cold bedroom.

I fished out my phone from inside my bag and texted Killian.

Me: *We're in.*

A moment passed.

Killian: *Good. Be safe.*

And that was it. No other answer, no other message. Just be safe. It was almost like saying, "I don't care about you. Go away."

At least that was how it felt.

I erased the messages—I planned on doing that every time I texted him, so if the witches ended up with my phone, they wouldn't be able to read them.

I sat on the bed and let out a long sigh. Evelyn and I had made it. We were inside.

And now began the hard part.

11

___

KNOWING THE WITCHES HERE WORE BALLGOWNS FOR breakfast, I couldn't choose anything less for a nighttime party. Cyrene said the closet would have some clothes, but she lied. It was crammed with all kinds of dresses and miles of dark fabrics.

And the scarier part: most of them fit me like a glove.

I tried on three before settling on a deep green one, the color of Killian's eyes, with a modest neckline and a low back. I applied some makeup and had my hair pulled into a loose braid over my shoulder.

Soon, Evelyn came. She wore a beautiful red gown with a wrapping of laces around her waist that twisted on the back and fell down like tails above the skirt.

"I wish Killian could see you," Evelyn said as we walked to the main hall. "He wouldn't be able to resist you."

I snorted. "Oh, believe me, he would. He has resisted me all along." I frowned. "Honestly, it doesn't seem that hard to him."

That thought brought a painful squeeze to my heart. As

much as I wanted him close to me, I couldn't take much more of this hot and cold thing. I wished he would go through with what I told him: he had to take the box to DuMoir Castle now and leave me behind. There was nothing he could do while I was in here. Better to take the box to safety.

Better to have him away so I wouldn't be tempted to think we could be more than a witch and a vampire who hated witches.

"He's a fool." Evelyn entwined her arm with mine. My back went still. "I'm usually not this friendly, you know. After years hiding and being on my own, I built a wall around me so tall and thick, I became grumpy and lonely. I never thought anyone could break through it. I didn't want anyone to break through."

"Then Asher came along," I said.

She nodded. "He did, and he disarmed me completely, as if crumbling my walls to dust was the easiest thing he had ever done." She glanced at me with her big, chocolate eyes. "I haven't had a real friend in quite a long time, but you've lived the same troubles I have, you like the same things I do. I feel like you understand me."

I raised my eyebrows at her. "Are you feeling okay?"

"Hm." She let out a little chuckle. "I might have had a drink or two while I was getting ready. I thought it was going to be good for my nerves. Now, I think I might have drunk too much."

I smiled. "As long as you can keep up our game while we're surrounded by dark witches."

She winked at me. "I think I can do that."

We turned a corner and saw more witches flocking toward the main hall.

"Just so you know, I haven't had a real friend before." I tugged on her arm. "I like this."

She smiled at me.

We joined the throng of witches entering the main hall. My steps faltered as I scanned around. There were easily two hundred witches in here. How the hell were we supposed to steal the box and the dragon bones and get out of here alive?

Just as I turned to ask Evelyn, Lorie and Keeva appeared at our side. They laced their arms on ours and now we were a link of four witches in ridiculously lavish gowns.

"I'm so glad you two passed the test," Lorie said. She had her long pipe in her hand, though it didn't seem lit at the moment.

"Me too." Keeva nodded. "We haven't had any tests in many years, and then boom, the two of you come and knock Cyrene's socks off. That was something."

I stared at Keeva. "You're saying we impressed Cyrene?"

"You sure did," Lorie said. "Though she'll never tell you that. Shit, don't let her know we told you that."

"Your secret is safe with us," Evelyn joked.

Lorie and Keeva laughed, pulling us around the main hall. A low rock ballad filled the air, along with the scent of cinnamon and vanilla—whatever was being cooked for dinner must be good. Black candles flickered from sconces placed on the wall every few feet, and from the big flower arrangements on the long tables. The light of the candles reflected on the giant glass walls like twinkling stars.

Lorie and Keeva guided us through the vast room, introducing us to every witch we passed. We met witches as young as twelve, and as old as two hundred and forty-seven. They told us only twelve or older were allowed at certain parties—most parties were for eighteen plus. I remembered how Lorie had grabbed a human and ridden him in the corner and understood why.

The younger witches were kept in a separate part of the lodge, being educated and raised by older witches. It sounded like an orphanage to me.

Most witches we met seemed skeptical of us, while only a handful seemed excited for new meat. I wished I could tell them not to worry, that we wouldn't be here long, but ... yeah, that wouldn't work out well.

A sudden hush fell over the room, and the witches turned to the main door. Cyrene walked in, followed by two Dark Order members. She wore a long, black dress with a skirt that parted in the middle, revealing tight pants and stilettos underneath. She stepped to the side and Princess Fabula entered the room, with four Dark Order soldiers behind her. The princess wore a dark gray gown with black diamonds peppering the skirt. A wreath of black diamonds adorned her neck and her wrist.

She smiled at the witches, who clapped and whistled.

"My beloved sisters," Princess Fabula began. "We're celebrating a special occasion tonight: We now have two new sisters, Lavinia and Evelyn."

The clapping started again. Evelyn and I waved at the witches, even though I knew most of them were rolling their eyes at us.

"Congratulations on passing the test, Lavinia and Evelyn. You're now and forever a part of the Nightmist coven." She grabbed a flute from one of the guards beside her—I hadn't even seen him holding it—and raised it high. "To our new sisters." The cheering rang loud for a few seconds. "Please, enjoy the party."

Cyrene and the Dark Order escorted Princess Fabula to

the table in the center, where a black chair had been placed at the head. One of the guards pulled the chair back and helped the princess down. Then Cyrene turned to us.

Lorie and Keeva pushed us forward. "Go," Lorie said.

"She's waiting for you," Keeva added.

My stomach knotted as Evelyn and I walked to Cyrene and Princess Fabula.

"The princess would like you two to sit with her," Cyrene said, gesturing to the two chairs to the left of the princess. I sat down, taking the seat closest to the princess, and Evelyn sat to my left. Her eyes always on us, Cyrene sat down at the princess's right.

As soon as the four of us were seated, the Dark Order formed a line behind the princess, and a girl appeared beside her. She looked meek and young, and human. She picked up small plates from the silver tray in her arms and placed them in front of us, starting with the princess. Then another girl replaced her and delivered us drinks—champagne.

I frowned. A comment about having human servants burned my tongue. Noticing what I was about to do, Evelyn discreetly kicked me under the table. When I looked up at her, she gave me a slight head shake.

Fine! I swallowed the comment, but that only weighed heavier inside me.

I had known these were dark witches. What had I been expecting? Kindness to us didn't redeem them.

I wasn't that stupid.

Princess Fabula tasted the hors d'oeuvres on her plate and sipped from her champagne. Meanwhile, Cyrene barely moved, her eyes switching from me to Evelyn, and back to me. Before, she had seemed easygoing, but now she was like a hawk, watching for threats.

She was the one we had to be most careful of.

"Taste this one." Fabula picked up a gray puff and placed it in her mouth. She moaned. "It's my favorite."

Evelyn and I obliged and I was surprised to find its bitter taste ended in a sweet note. It really was good.

I frowned and glanced around at the witches mingling together, dancing, chatting, laughing, eating, drinking. They looked so normal, so friendly. Were we sure these were dark witches?

A line of human men walked into the main hall, wearing nothing more than leather boxers. Some had chains around their arms, others were holding whips and other sex toys.

My stomach revolved and the little food I had eaten so far felt heavy.

The men spread out as the witches advanced on them, and in no time, there were witches pushing the men down on chairs right in the middle of the room and straddling them— once more having sex in plain sight.

My cheeks heated and I averted my eyes, though I couldn't clamp my ears and not listen to their moans.

Princess Fabula chuckled. "You'll get used to it." She leaned forward. "Maybe you'll even participate."

The heat in my cheeks increased. "We'll see," was all I said.

"Oh, there they are," Princess Fabula said. She smiled and stared toward the doors.

I followed her line of sight. Three men, exuding power and confidence, entered the ballroom dressed in tailored suits. Witches stopped to look at them, while others fanned themselves as they walked past.

They strolled directly to our table and stopped beside the princess and Cyrene.

"Good evening," one of them said to everyone. He looked like the oldest of the trio, probably about twenty-six or seven years old. His dark blond hair was cut short and his dark-brown eyes reminded me of someone.

The other two greeted us too, though they seemed bored. I narrowed my eyes, staring at them. One of the two others was like younger version of the oldest, and the other had light blond hair curling around his ears and gray eyes.

"My darling." Princess Fabula turned to Evelyn and me. "These are my sons, Heath and Deron." She gestured to the oldest guy and his younger copy.

"And Tade here is my son," Cyrene said, pointing to the third one.

Now I understood why they reminded of someone—*someones*. They looked a lot like their mothers.

"Nice to meet you," Heath said, bowing his head slightly.

"Likewise," I said at the same time Evelyn said, "You too."

Deron and Tade mumbled something, but still looked like they wanted to be anywhere else but here.

"Forgive Deron and Tade," Princess Fabula said. "They would rather be in their uniforms and with the rest of the Dark Order instead of enjoying a party."

"It's what we're trained for," Deron said, his voice tight.

"We're in a building full of powerful witches," Cyrene said. "You can take a night off. Besides, if something happens, I know you can fight just as well in your suits."

They nodded, looking smug.

"Heath." Princess Fabula reached for her oldest son. He caught her hand in his. "And Tade. Why don't you two take Lavinia and Evelyn for a dance?"

I froze. "Hm, it's okay, Princess Fabu—"

"Oh, please, call me Fabula," she said, her tone friendly

but with no room for negotiation. She let go of Heath's hand, reached over the table, and squeezed my hand for three seconds. She frowned for a brief moment, and then smiled at me again. "We're among friends here, my darling." She looked at Heath. "Go."

Heath let go of his mother's hand, walked around her chair, and offered his hand to me. "Would you do me the honor?"

No, I didn't want to. But how could I say no to the princess's son in front of her? Shit. I slipped my hand in his and stood. I let him guide us back to an open area between the long tables, where other witches and humans danced.

I glanced over my shoulder and saw Tade and Evelyn right behind us. I was a single woman, but I would bet Asher wouldn't like his girl dancing with another man, even if it was for an undercover mission.

Heath halted at the center of the improvised dance floor and faced me. He turned my hand in his and placed his free hand on my waist. "Is this okay?"

I frowned. He was probably used to the witches having sex on the table during dinnertime, and yet he asked if having his hand on my waist was okay.

"Yes," I muttered.

We started moving. Heath took the lead, twirling us around the dance floor, matching the song's beat, even though it was a slow rock ballad and not a waltz.

Our bodies pressed close, and it was hard not to look at him. I glanced up and found he was staring at me. Defiance flickered in me and held his gaze. I had to admit, he was handsome. Freckles dotted his sharp nose and high cheekbones. He was tall and broad—not as tall as Killian, but slightly broader. Why the hell was I comparing this man to that vampire?

I shook my head.

"Something wrong?" Heath asked.

"No, nothing wrong." This was the princess's son. I had to make sure he had no reason to tell her I was a bitch or that he was suspicious of me. I had to be friendly. "I'm just overwhelmed."

"Oh, yes, I heard you and your friend haven't been around witches much," he noted. His eyes scanned the sides for three seconds before returning to mine. "Usually, witches are eccentric and boisterous. And these ones take the trophy for being loud and loving a good party."

I couldn't help but smile. "You must be proud to be able to protect them."

He leaned closer, and my stomach tightened. "Can I tell you a secret? When I was younger, I hated all of this. The parties, the drinking, the cackles ..." Just then, a loud laugh echoed through the ballroom and he raised his eyebrows at me. My smile widened. "I didn't want anything to do with them."

My smile faded. "What changed?"

"When I was a teenager, the Brotherhood of Purity set a trap for our witches," he said, his voice low, hard. "We lost many witches that day, and some Dark Order members too. My father was one of them. And the Brotherhood almost killed my mother. That day, I vowed I would work harder than anyone to make sure she was always safe."

That was noble. "That's why it upsets you to be here as a guest of the party, and not as a warrior?"

His chin dipped. "Yes, but my mother insisted tonight."

"Sorry you had to go through that."

His hand slipped from the side of my waist to my lower back, bringing me closer to him. I inhaled deeply. "I'm not sorry anymore."

Oh!

Warmth spread over my cheeks for the thousandth time in the last hour.

I averted my eyes and saw the tiger lounging at the entrance. I stiffened. "The tiger is a familiar?"

Heath looked at the animal. "Yes, my mother's. But don't worry. He's loyal to my mother and wouldn't attack anyone she didn't order him to. You're safe."

"That's good to know." I thought for a second. "And Cyrene has a raven." He nodded. It made sense since only the strongest of the light and dark witches had familiars. "Who else has familiars?"

"Lorie has a small green lizard, but that's it."

So the three of them were the strongest witches here. Interesting. Something else poked at my mind. "I heard dark witches usually have a council under the princess."

"That's true, but my mother doesn't have an official council. She trusts Cyrene, and a handful of others, like Lorie, Keeva, and Dot. When needed, she calls on them. Otherwise, she rules alone."

"She's awe-inspiring," I said, glancing at where Fabula sat at the table's head, talking to Cyrene. It wasn't a total lie, because she really struck me as strong and far from ordinary, but I only said that to gain some points.

His lips tugged up. "She really is."

We continued dancing and talking. Heath was now the captain of the Dark Order, and he was recruiting more members. Unfortunately, witches didn't get pregnant easily, and when they did, most of their babies were females, not males. And sometimes, the males didn't want to be a part of a magical life when they didn't possess magic themselves, and they left. Thus why their numbers were so low.

"But ... is there a need for the Dark Order?" I asked, genuinely curious. "I mean, like Princess Fabula said—"

"Don't let her hear you calling her princess when she specifically told you not to. She'll take that as disrespect, like you don't care for her wishes."

"Right. Hm. As I was saying ... Fabula said the witches are all powerful here. No one would dare come against them."

"The Brotherhood would," Heath said, sure of himself.

Right. So far, the Brotherhood sounded like the true evil, even though they claimed to have been chosen by God.

The scent of butter and sweet potatoes reached my nose and I turned to the tables. Human females brought out individual plates and placed them on the tables. The witches started moving to take their places.

Heath placed my hand in the crook of his elbow, guiding me back to my seat. Evelyn was already back—I hadn't even seen her leaving the dance floor—and Tade sat on her left. Deron was seated across the table, beside Cyrene, and Heath sat at his brother's right, his eyes on me.

I looked down at my hands folded in my lap before anyone else saw my pink cheeks.

Evelyn nudged me with her elbow. Yeah, there was no fooling her. She raised her eyebrows at me, and I offered her a forced smile. "Are you okay?" she asked in a whisper while the witches began eating.

Not trusting my voice, I nodded.

The first course was roasted carrots and sweet potatoes seasoned in butter and herbs. I wasn't a fan of carrots, but I had to admit, this dish was delicious.

Dinner went on with a five-course meal and lots of small talk, and ended with a savory and warm dulce de leche cake topped with salted caramel—divine!

"When you were dancing with my son," Fabula started, talking to me, "Evelyn told me she was born to dark witches and was hunted by light witches and the Brotherhood. She also told me you don't know which coven your mother was from."

I nodded. "She never told me, and then she died and I had no way of finding out."

"What's your mother's name?"

"Zaira."

Fabula's eyes widened. "Oh ... that can't be." Fabula turned to Cyrene. "Zaira."

Cyrene froze, her fork with the last bite of cake stopped midair. She lowered her fork. "Are you sure that was her name?"

I almost rolled my eyes. I think I would know my mother's name. "Yes. Why?"

Fabula glanced at me, a soft gleam in her eyes. "Darling. About twenty-some years ago, a witch named Zaira disappeared from our coven."

I sucked in a sharp breath. No, that couldn't be. Queen Denise had said I wasn't a light or dark witch. My mother couldn't be from Nightmist ... I stared at them, at a loss.

Beside me, Evelyn was as rigid as I was, though her expression didn't show any emotion at all.

Cyrene nodded. "We thought the Brotherhood had taken her. We went after them, but lost track."

"That was a horrible day. I mourned for months. And now I know she truly passed away." Fabula placed a hand over her chest. "My darling, your mother was my best friend."

My jaw worked. Open, close. Open, close. But no words came out.

"How do you know it's the same witch?" Evelyn asked.

Fabula chuckled. "A witch named Zaira who disappeared twenty plus years ago." She stared at me. "And now that I know that, I can see Zaira in you. In your hazel eyes, in your dark hair. You look a lot like her."

I swallowed hard. I knew I looked like her. When I was little, everyone called me her mini-me. I had only a handful of pictures, but even I could see I had turned out to be her twin.

But that couldn't be. Because if it was true, then it meant my mother was a dark witch.

I was a dark witch.

Dot walked by the table and Fabula hailed her.

"Yes, my princess?" Dot asked.

"Remember Zaira? A witch with wild dark hair and an air element gift?"

Dot's eyes rounded. "Of course I do."

Fabula pointed at me. "This is her daughter."

Dot's jaw fell open. "No way!" A smile stretched over from ear to ear. "And you came to us without knowing it? This is fate!"

They called other witches over and soon the entire room knew I was Zaira's daughter. Most witches had been with the coven when my mother was here, and they all seemed to love her.

"Zaira was the best of all of us."

"She had the best gift."

"Yes, she always blew wind at our faces!

"She was so pretty."

"Yeah, but she had that little scar above her left eyebrow."

"Oh, I remember how she got that."

And on and on, they went.

Some witches hugged me, content I had found them, and others cried on my shoulder, saying they had hoped my mother was alive and happy somewhere, but now they knew she was gone.

My mind spun, and I felt dizzy and confused.

Suddenly, Heath appeared by my side and offered his arm to me. "Walk with me." The witches stared at us, interest clear in their eyes, while Fabula smiled at us. Evelyn, though, stared at me as if I was crazy. Heath leaned closer and whispered, "I'm trying to save you here."

Instantly, I placed my hand on his arm, letting him guide me out of the main hall.

Once we were alone in the near dark hallways, I inhaled deeply. "Thank you."

"No worries. I saw how overwhelmed you were."

I nodded. "It's a lot to take in."

We crossed under a doorway and stepped into the lobby. The fireplace was still burning, the fire high and hot, and outside, the stars twinkled in the dark sky.

"Aren't you happy, though? You found out your mother was from our coven, the coven you just joined." He halted a few feet in front of the fireplace, the flames casting golden shadows on his face. "Fate."

I stared at the crinkling fire. "I am happy," I lied. "Just overwhelmed."

He nodded. "I bet."

A sudden thought populated my mind and I inhaled deeply. "Heath, do you know if my mother had any sisters?

Or if her mother is still here?" If I had a relative in the coven, there was a way of breaking the blood promise!

"As far as I know, Zaira was an only child, and her mother died when she was young." He paused. "I'm sorry."

Damn it. I hadn't been counting on finding my mother's relatives, but for those three seconds when I believed it was possible, hope had filled my veins so fast ... Apparently, I was destined to never have this damn blood promise broken.

"It's okay," I muttered. I shoved thoughts of blood promises away from my mind. I wasn't here for that.

"Come on. I'll escort you to your bedroom."

This time, he didn't offer me his arm and I was grateful for that. We walked in silence until we were in front of my bedroom's door.

I turned to him. "Thank you for the rescue."

One corner of his lips curled up. "My pleasure." He bowed his head once, then spun, and walked away.

I watched his back for a couple of seconds, then slipped into my bedroom and locked the door behind me.

Oh my God! I pressed a hand to my chest and took in several deep breaths, trying to calm myself down.

This was too much.

My mother, a Nightmist witch?

That was crazy.

But it wasn't a coincidence.

What was it then? Fate?

I sank on my bed and buried my face in my hands.

No ... I couldn't be a dark witch.

Could I?

12

AFTER A FREAK-OUT MOMENT, I CHANGED OUT OF MY DRESS and put on leggings, a thin sweater, and boots. I turned on the lamps beside the bed, turned off the overhead light, sat on my bed, and waited—my mind blank. I didn't want to think of anything right now.

As agreed, Evelyn came into my room at three in the morning. Like me, she had changed into more comfortable clothes.

She sat beside me. "How are you?"

"How do you think?" I glanced at her, my eyes hard. "I'm lost and confused and ... I don't even know."

"You didn't believe them, did you?"

I startled. "Why would I not? They knew her appearance, they knew about her gift." Which I didn't know before, but now I could see it clear in my head now. She had used it many times before, to blow my hair or push me somewhere when I didn't want to move ... I just hadn't realized it. "They knew about her scar." They couldn't have come up with that. "It *is* my mother."

"So what?"

"Excuse me?"

"I'm born from light witches, but I have a dark witch's magic. Some people labeled me dark witch, plain and simple. But I still know that these witches are evil, and even though I'm the same kind, I don't want any association with them." She paused. "And you can make the same choice."

Oh, my damn head hurt.

I shoved it to the back of my mind, instead focusing on why we were here: the box and the dragon bones. Even if these witches weren't evil as we first thought, Evelyn still needed the dragon bones, and I still agreed with Killian that no one should possess the boxes and abuse them. We needed to take these two items out of here.

I stood. "All right. Let's do what we came to do."

In silence, Evelyn and I sneaked out of my bedroom and down the dark hallway. The only light came from moonlight streaming through the glass walls and windows and a few lamps in the common areas. We were as quiet as we could because we knew not all the witches were sleeping—some had invited the humans back to their bedrooms—and I bet the Dark Order had some kind of patrol around the lodge.

So, we practically tiptoed down to the first floor, dodging the Dark Order and drunk witches. At one point, we almost came face-to-face with Dot and her human as she rode him on a chaise lounge in the lobby. I made a mental note to never sit on that chaise.

And then we almost bumped into Heath and Tade while they patrolled the hallway leading to Fabula's throne room.

Shit, maybe we should have chosen another night to try this.

Finally, we stopped in front of the metal door with the big lock.

"How do we get in?" I whispered.

Evelyn winked at me. She pulled out a vial from her utility belt. She opened it and put the douser right inside the lock. She let two drops fall and pulled it back. A moment later, a soft click sounded. I gasped at her. With a winning smile, she turned the lock and the door swung open.

We went in and closed the door behind us.

For a moment, we were bathed in darkness.

My heart sped in my chest.

Then moonlight glittered from the thin glass window near the tall ceiling and my eyes adjusted to the near darkness.

A large room extended in front of us, with a long wooden table, a few chairs, and behind it, wooden shelves filled with old books, vials with liquids of every color imaginable, herb powders, and ... holy shit, bat wings, rat tails, and more disgusting things in large glass vials.

I frowned as I walked around the shelves. The box and the dragon bones had to be here, right? If they were inside this lodge, this was the room to hide them, right?

I scanned the shelves ... I found a glass jar with small marble balls and colored light swirling inside them; a dried hand and arm, which had to be a fake; a tall candle, thicker than my arm, with a dark flame that didn't seem to burn; small vials with skull labels; several tarot decks with golden trimmed cards; palm-sized purple leaves with white and silver lines; and so much more. This was like a treasure trove, albeit a creepy one.

"I found them!" Evelyn said in a loud whisper.

I rushed to her. She stood between two tall shelves, an open wooden box in her hands. Inside, I could see long, sharp teeth. I gasped. "Are these ... dragon teeth?"

She nodded. "This is what I was looking for. Have you found yours?"

"Not yet."

She closed the box and hugged it tight. "What does it look like?"

"A black rectangular stone." I moved my hands to show her the size. "It doesn't look like a box."

Evelyn's eyes moved up and down the shelf. "Let's keep looking."

Since she was here, I walked to the next shelf and scanned the items again. The box wasn't small, but it could be easily lost among so many items, especially if the witches had gotten it, but didn't know what it could do.

The sound of heels clicking on the wooden floors echoed from the door.

"Shit," I muttered.

Evelyn raced to me and both of us crouched behind the last shelf before the back wall.

Fabula entered the room, with Cyrene right behind her. The raven flew in too, and perched on top of a short shelf by the door. What the hell were they doing here at this time of the night?

"I told you, I can't shake it," Fabula said. She stopped before the long table and turned to her second in command. "I had this vivid dream ... something in here is more powerful than we know." She spun on her heels and looked at the shelves. "I don't just know what."

"I hear you, but couldn't this have waited until morning?" Cyrene ran a hand over her messy blond bob. The top part of her gown was unlaced, as if she had put it back in a hurry. "It's not like this mysterious item could disappear from this room at will."

"You never know." Fabula took a step closer to the shelves. "After all, these are all magical items."

Cyrene groaned. "So what will you do? Test all of them to see which one you dreamed about? Right now?"

Fabula sighed. "No, of course not. It's just ..." She pressed a hand to her chest. "There was such a sense of urgency to it." She walked between two shelves and rifled through items.

"We need to go," I whispered to Evelyn.

She glanced at the box in her hands. "Damn it." She carefully placed the dragon teeth box on the shelf in front of us. Good call. We had to leave it here until we were able to retrieve both items. If one disappeared before the other, it would create a bigger mess.

Evelyn took a small rock from the shelf and threw it in the other corner of the room.

The noise of the rock hitting the wall echoed through the room.

"What was that?" Fabula asked.

"Who's there?" Cyrene advanced toward the sound.

The raven flew toward it.

"Now!" I ran to the door, as silently as I could, with Evelyn right on my tail. We exited through the metal door and stopped short as the tiger crossed the hallway in the opposite direction.

These damn familiars!

Evelyn and I plastered to the wall, barely breathing, until we were sure the tiger was gone. Didn't he have good hearing and senses? Damn, we had to be more careful.

Slowly, we advanced to the corner of the hallway, where it

intersected with another. We glanced side to side, but there was no one there. We ran again.

As we approached the stairs, voices reached us. We hid in a small alcove outside the music room, waiting to see where the voices were coming from and going.

"—she's in way over her head," a female voice said, a groan in her words.

"I know, but we'll deal with her," another one said, equally agitated.

I focused and realized the voices were coming from the storage room across the hallway. The door was almost closed, but when I leaned closer, I could see the silhouette of two witches.

"Did you see how she fawned over the new witches? What was up with that?"

New witches? That would be Evelyn and me. We exchanged a look.

"Let her be. That's just Fabula being Fabula."

"You mean soft and weak. She needs to be gone."

"She will. In time, she will."

What the …

Footsteps approached and the two witches closed the door with a soft click. Evelyn and I ducked into the alcove again and held our breath. The footsteps got closer, but then turned a corner and went in another direction.

I exhaled. "Damn, that is too close. We need to go back to our bedroom ASAP."

"I know."

We looked side to side before continuing our way, but right before we reached the stairs, the footsteps were back. Evelyn and I rushed into the first open door we saw—the kitchen.

The footsteps grew louder.

"Act natural," I told her as I opened the fridge, grabbed a beer bottle, and handed it to her. Then I grabbed an hors d'oeuvre from the box beside the fridge and shoved it in my mouth.

Evelyn uncapped the beer and took a sip.

A second later, Heath and Tade walked into the kitchen. They turned on the lights and I blinked with the sudden brightness. The two soldiers narrowed their eyes at us.

"What's going on here?" Tade asked, clearly suspicious.

"Sorry." I picked up another hors d'oeuvre and showed it to them. "I know this is not the best time, but we were hungry."

"Didn't you eat at the party?" Heath asked.

"We were too nervous." Evelyn reached across the counter and got an hors d'oeuvre for herself. "Now it's catching up to us."

They stared at us while we ate. Evelyn took another sip of the beer.

"All right," Heath said. "Grab a plate, fill it with food, and then let's go. We'll escort you back to your bedrooms."

"Oh, we don't want to impose," I said, batting my lashes like I used to do with Rex. It had worked with him, but he was a half-goblin, half-fae. Maybe it wouldn't work with male witches who became badass warriors.

"It's no problem," Tade said, his voice tight.

Evelyn and I found plates in the cabinets and filled them with enough hors d'oeuvres to last several days, then we turned to the two men.

"Ready?" Heath asked.

"Yup," I said. Evelyn put more hors d'oeuvre in her mouth and nodded.

Tate took the lead. "Let's go."

As we exited the kitchen, Evelyn leaned closer to me and whispered, "Next time, find me wine or whiskey. I hate beer."

Despite the situation, I chuckled.

13

IT TOOK ME A LONG TIME TO SLEEP BECAUSE: ONE, WE WERE IN a different place, undercover among what were supposed to be evil witches. Two, I couldn't stop thinking about the fact that my mother had been a Nightmist witch and voilà, here I was. Was it coincidence or fate? And three, I was certain Fabula and Cyrene would burst into my bedroom at any moment.

Plus, I couldn't shake what Evelyn and I had overheard. Two witches talking about getting rid of Fabula? What had that been about?

When I woke up a handful of hours later, I felt like a truck had run me over. I was tired, hungry, and grumpy. If we weren't on a mission, I would have told these witches to flip off and slept some more.

Instead, I flung my covers aside, took a quick shower, and put on the simplest black dress in my closet—and still, I looked ready for a cocktail party. I tied my wild hair in a ponytail, applied some makeup to hide the black bags under my eyes, and reported for breakfast with Evelyn. There was no set structure to the witches' day, but Cyrene had told us last night that they always had much to do. She asked that we report to the lobby after breakfast, where a witch would be waiting for us.

"There you are," Hester said when Evelyn and I arrived. We had met her last night during the party, but after so many introductions, it was a miracle I remembered her name. "Come with me."

A short witch with round cheeks and small eyes took us through a set of corridors to a sunroom—a balcony jutting from the lodge over the mountainside, with glass walls and ceilings. I squinted at the brightness of the sun filtering through the glass, but gasped at the set up in front of me.

Long tables spread over the place, with all kinds of alchemy and apothecary equipment—mortar and pestles, scrapers, knives, scales, jars, chemistry tubes, and more. Witches with gloves, goggles, and aprons worked with herbs and liquids, chopping, measuring, mixing ...

"Potions," I whispered.

"Yes," Hester said, her tone flat. "Fabula was delighted to find out you two shared an interest in potions. She thought you would like to work here."

Fabula knew we liked potions? I glanced to Evelyn.

"I mentioned it to her when you were dancing with Heath," Evelyn said.

Ah.

A witch with dark skin and short black hair approached us.

"This is Peony," Hester said. I remembered meeting her during the party, but I was glad Hester mentioned her name, because I didn't remember that. "She'll show you around and then give you a task."

"Come with me," Peony said.

"Thank you," I told Hester as we followed Peony to one of the low tables.

Hester didn't pay me any attention as she turned and left.

Peony stopped beside the table, where dozens of small glass cups contained all kinds of herbs. She gestured to the cups. "There are two hundred and thirty-seven different herbs on the table. Tell me the name and purpose of all of them."

I stared at her. What the hell?

Evelyn didn't waste time. She started with the one on the right corner and worked her way to the left, naming all the herbs.

Peony raised a manicured eyebrow at me.

Shit. I went to the opposite corner and pointed to the first herb on the left. I opened my mouth and—

"Lavinia."

I whirled around and found Cyrene at the room's entrance. "Yes?"

"Come with me," was all she said before walking away.

I glanced at Evelyn, but she was lost in the herbs. I looked at Peony. Should I ask for permission to go? She waved me off before I could say anything, and I rushed after Cyrene.

Without a word, she took me to the throne room. There, Fabula stood beside the couch to the right, while Deron and another Dark Order soldier remained stationed at her chair in the back of the room.

She saw me come in and smiled at me. "My darling, there you are. Did you sleep well?"

I frowned. So Heath and Tade hadn't told her about my kitchen raid last night. That was a relief.

"I did," I said.

"Good, good." She walked toward me, then waved Cyrene off. The witch bowed her head and marched out of the room. "First, I had planned for you and Evelyn to work in the potions' room, but after learning about your mother ..." She looked at me, affection clear in her eyes. "I thought I should train you myself."

I opened my mouth. Closed it again. Finally, I said, "I'm not particularly good, Fabula. My mother died when I was eleven. I never had proper training."

"But now you will." She cupped my elbow and pulled me forward. "And while we train, I can tell you more about your mother."

My chest seized and emotion clogged my throat. This sounded ... like a dream. "I would like that."

<hr>

THE HOURS PASSED IN A FLASH. Thank goodness I had drunk one of Evelyn's special potions that morning that gave me fake magic for a few hours so I could trick Fabula; otherwise, she would be showing me tricks and spells, and I wouldn't be able to replicate any of it.

As it was, I could do most of it. Though even I could see she was starting with small things like conjuring a small ball of magic, stretching it into a thin line, curling back into a ball, throwing it from hand to hand without touching, then up and down, then around me in a circle, and finally, making bigger bolts and throwing them at a target—a cylinder-shaped dummy taller than me that Heath had brought in.

Meanwhile, Fabula told me about my mother.

Fabula was a handful of years older than my mother, but my

mother had always been mature for her age and ended up with many older friends. And the closest was Fabula. Back then, they lived in northern United States, in a manor surrounded by farms. Even though the witches were told to keep to themselves, Fabula and my mother never sat still. They sneaked out to the farms and played with the animals, especially the chickens. They went into the chicken coop and zapped their feet, making them jump high, higher than they thought possible, which made them laugh and do it again. Once, they didn't stop until the chickens were mad and exhausted—and some of them jumped the fence ... it was a chicken run.

"We didn't know if we should fall down laughing, hide, or go after the chickens," Fabula said.

"What did you do?"

"We were young and irresponsible and afraid of consequences, so we hid. But the farmer knew it had been us, so even though he despised stepping foot on our lands, he came over to complain. My mother was princess back then, and she scared the poor man away. But she punished your mother and me. We had to hand wash all the curtains in the manor. I don't remember now how many there were, but let me tell you, it took us *days* to wash them all."

Next, she told me about the time they stole a car and went to the nearest city to the movies and a nightclub. They had been twelve and seventeen. The movies, they went in all right. But the nightclub? They had to spell the bouncer, and inside, people kept asking their age and saying they were too young to be in there. They ended up spelling almost everyone inside the nightclub.

But Fabula's mother found out, of course, and this time, she made the two girls polish the floors of the entire manor and wash the windows. Fabula said they hated it, but they always made a game out of their punishments and had fun.

I gobbled up every word, every story, entranced in this figure, in this image of the person my mother had been. Fabula made her sound so carefree and cool, I wish I had been her friend back then.

At some point, lunch was brought over, then an afternoon snack. Cyrene came in a few times with short reports, the Dark Order members changed, and somehow I had spent the entire day practicing magic and talking about my mother.

For dinner, Fabula asked me to leave. "I'm sorry, my darling, but I really need to talk with Cyrene."

"Of course," I said, only a little sad about leaving her.

"But tomorrow morning, come back. We'll practice more."

I smiled at her and practically skipped out of the room.

Until I came face-to-face with Evelyn who descended the stairs. Her brows slammed down when she saw me. "What are you smiling about?"

My shoulders sagged. Shit. I had forgotten about everything—the box, the mission, and Killian. But who could blame me? It wasn't every day you met your dead mother's best friend.

"Nothing," I said quick. Too quick.

Evelyn glanced over my shoulder to the door at the end of the corridor—Fabula's throne room. "I see you have a new bestie."

I frowned. "Don't say that. You know how delicate this is."

She walked up to me and lowered her voice as she said, "All I know is that you're letting yourself be enchanted by something that might be a lie." I flinched. It wasn't a lie. I was sure of it. "Focus on what we have to do here."

Evelyn marched to the main hall for dinner.

Suddenly not hungry, I climbed the stairs and went to my bedroom. I plopped on my bed and rubbed the heels of my palms on my eyes.

What the hell was happening here?

There was no way I could erase from my mind that my mother was a Nightmist witch, that she had grown up with most of these witches, that I was one of them.

The other thing that was throwing me off was the witches per se. Despite being loud, a little crazy, and sometimes a little vulgar, they were normal. Like, not evil. At least, they seemed to be. Fabula doted on the witches, she held her sons' hands affectionately, and she really seemed touched I was here.

I picked up my phone from the nightstand, glancing at the screen. No new messages, no calls. Nothing from Killian.

Evelyn and I agreed that if we didn't make it out in seven days, we would meet the guys at the inn to regroup.

That meant six more days here, without Killian. But I felt restless. I needed to see him.

Right now.

14

T HANKFULLY, I HAD A FEW OF EVELYN'S INVISIBILITY POTIONS. She had made a bunch before we came, just in case.

Perhaps seeing Killian was a waste of a potion, but I couldn't help it. Despite his irritating mood the last time I had seen him, he was the only anchor left to my life in Forest Creek. The only thing that connected me to my past, the only person who knew who I had been before.

For some reason, I thought seeing him would bring me clarity of mind. That it would help organize the jumble of thoughts. It would make me realize how stupid I was being.

Knowing Evelyn would come for me later so we could explore the lodge and try to find the box again, I sent her a text, telling her I was meeting Killian. I thought she would see it and stop me, but she either didn't see it, or she didn't care.

I knew she was mad at me for waffling like this, but I couldn't help it!

Fifteen minutes before one in the morning, I changed into leggings, a sweater, a thick jacket, beanie, gloves, and boots to stave off the frozen night. After drinking the potion, I exited the lodge like a ghost, but I wasn't soundless. I crept down the hallways, spotted guards and familiars, and opened and closed a sliding door leading to the balcony outside. I held my breath, afraid someone would see through the spell. I mean, we were inside a lodge full of witches—someone could undo the spell.

To my relief, no one saw me or heard me, and under the falling snow, I followed the fence line, like Killian and I had done the first time we had come here, to hide my footprints.

In the distance, I saw the tiger patrolling the area. At some point, he turned my way and I thought he had heard me. I stopped, my breath slow and shallow. He came closer, but changed directions before he came too near. I exhaled once he was out of sight. I only had a few minutes left with this damn potion. If I didn't make it to the trees in time, I would be seen, I was sure of it.

I got to the trees but didn't slow down. I followed the woods, my eyes on the road to my left. A car was parked behind a line of thick trees—a black pickup truck—I felt the shimmer of the magic fading.

I approached the car and saw Killian, bathed in darkness, behind the steering wheel. The magic flickered, revealing me. His eyes snapped in my direction. I raced to the car, slipping into the passenger seat.

I took off my beanie, shook the snow from my hair, and rubbed my hands together, glad for the heat. I turned to him. "You switched cars."

Killian watched me with hooded eyes. "I thought it was time." He wrapped his hands around the wheel. "Ready?"

I grabbed the seatbelt. "Yeah."

He peeled away from the grass and followed the narrow

road back to town. He drove slow in the snow—and silently. Now that I was with him, I was reconsidering this. Why had I come? To sit in uncomfortable silence? To get upset about his bad mood, which apparently hadn't changed since the last time I saw him?

I almost told him to forget about it, to take me back to the lodge, but I couldn't. A part of me wanted to be here, near him, with him, even if he was a pain in my ass.

Killian took the long way to the inn, circling around, and zigzagging through side roads. I didn't ask, but it was probably to make sure we weren't being followed.

The inn was quiet when we arrived, and our room looked exactly the same. I turned on the lamp on the nightstand and started pacing between the two queen beds. Killian closed the door, locked it, and leaned against it.

He looked immaculate in black jeans and a thin long-sleeved Henley shirt, while I probably looked on the precipice of madness.

Killian crossed his arms. "What's the problem?"

I continued pacing. "I don't even know where to begin."

"Just ... begin with something. Blurt out the first thing that comes to mind."

"I missed you." The words were out before I could make sense of them. I stopped short, pressing a hand to my mouth. Killian's brows slammed down and his jaw ticked with pressure. "I mean ..." Shit. "Why haven't you left? I told you to leave."

"You said that in the spur of the moment. We had made a plan before that and I stuck to it."

Right. Besides stoic and serious, he was also disciplined. He followed the plan to the end. So, I blurted out the next thing I wanted to talk to him about. "I found out my mother was one of them."

Killian's eyes rounded. "What?"

I sat down on the edge of my bed. "I know. It sounds crazy. And a crazy coincidence. But my mother was a Nightmist witch. They all remember her, her appearance, even the scar she had right here." I touched the upper side of my left eyebrow. "They keep telling me stories about her and how great she was, and—"

"Wait." Killian pushed away from the door. "You're not changing your mind about these witches, are you?"

I stared at him, not sure what to say. So far, I hadn't seen anything out of the unusual—besides all the let's-have-sex-right-here thing. Which was probably normal to them. But other than that? They seemed normal, friendly, caring ... at least toward one another. They seemed loyal and dedicated.

Evil? I didn't think so.

Killian gaped at me. "You can't be serious. These are dark witches!"

I shot to my feet. "I know! But even Evelyn possesses dark magic and she's not evil. And remember the demon hunters? They now know not all supernaturals are evil, not even demons." I paused. "What if these witches possess what is called dark magic, but they aren't evil?"

Killian ran a hand through his hair. "What are you saying? That you're changing your mind? That you're ... what? Staying here with them? That you're not going to steal the box anymore?"

"I don't know!" I shouted, but then caught myself. Last thing I needed was for another guest to complain about the noise. "I don't know," I repeated, softer. "I ... I feel lost and confused. Put yourself in my shoes, Killian. I barely knew my mother. She died when I was young. What kind of person, or witch, was she? And these witches are telling me about her." I exhaled. "It's like ... this was my mother's home before she met my father. Maybe it could be mine too."

Killian turned his back to me and marched to the opposite wall, as if he needed more distance from me.

That hurt.

Now I knew coming here had been the wrong thing to do.

"Never mind," I said, walking to the door. "I'll steal the box, give it to Evelyn, and she can bring it to you."

"What? No. Wait." He took two steps toward me.

Hand on the door's knob, I glanced at him.

"You're staying there?" he asked.

"I thought you would be happy," I said, my tone harsher than I ever intended. "This way, you don't have to deal with me anymore."

"What are you talking about?"

I gaped at him. Was he really going to make me say it? It didn't matter. The rage expanded in my chest and it wanted out! "You're distant. You avoid me, and when you aren't, you argue about the stupidest things. I think ... I think you regret asking me to come with you to DuMoir Castle."

He stared at me as if I was crazy. "That's not true."

"Then why the hell do I feel like you would rather be anywhere but with me?"

I blinked and he was right in front of me, his body inches from mine, his head slightly lowered and closer, his green eyes on mine. I plastered my back to the door and swallowed hard.

"Lavinia," Killian whispered, his voice rough, pained.

I shivered.

He stepped into me, pressing his entire body to mine.

I sucked in a sharp breath.

"I don't just want to be near you." His hands rested on my hips, his mouth hovering over my ear.

Butterflies took off in my stomach and I found it hard to breathe.

"I want to be *with* you. All the freaking time." He slid his hands up, inched his fingers under my sweater, caressed the skin of my lower back. Oh, God ... "I want you like I have never wanted anything or anyone else." He dipped lower, his mouth tracing a line down my neck.

I clutched his shoulders, holding on for dear life.

"I want you," he repeated, bringing his mouth around my jaw. "You drive me crazy."

I stilled, sensing a but in there. "But?"

Half a second later, Killian stood several feet away, black lines around his darkening green eyes, and his fangs show-ing. "But you're a *witch*."

I flinched. "I thought you had moved past that."

"Me too." He inhaled deeply. The black lines and the fangs disappeared. "But with Evelyn around ... Now you're talking about staying with Nightmist, and I can smell their foul magic on you!"

My heart squeezed and my eyes welled. "Don't worry," I said, my voice breaking. "I won't bother you anymore."

Before my knees gave out or I started crying in front of him, I opened the door and rushed out.

"Lavinia, wait!" he called after I closed the door behind me.

I marched down the corridor, down the stairs, and for some silly reason, I thought he was going to come to me, to catch up with me and tell me he was being ridiculous. That he didn't care I was a witch. That he still wanted me.

I gasped when he did appear in front of me with his damn super speed, and almost skidded in the parking lot's snow. Thankfully, I didn't fall on my butt.

I opened my mouth to tell him to leave me alone, but he raised both hands. "Wait. I know you won't let me take you back, but you can't walk there in the snow by yourself."

Shit, I had been so mad at him, I hadn't thought about that. The lodge was several miles from the inn, up the mountain, and it was still snowing.

"Here." He fished something out of his pocket and offered it to me. "Drive the truck yourself. Leave the keys inside and I'll retrieve it later."

I narrowed my eyes at his hand and the keys. Was this some sort of trick? I sighed. No. Despite everything, and despite being serious and stoic most of the time, Killian was a gentleman. He had left me in the dark alone before, and he had promised to never do that again.

I snatched the keys from him and swallowed the urge to say thank you. He didn't need my thanks. Without another glance, I walked past him. I hopped in the truck, turned the engine on, and drove away.

Finally, a tear escaped free.

Then another.

An another.

This time, I had left Killian behind.

But I had left my heart with him.

15

ON MY WAY BACK, THE TIGER ALMOST CAUGHT ME OUTSIDE, AND then Deron inside the lodge. My heart hammered as I lay in bed. And then came the anger and sadness. My eyes welled again, but I refused to cry. Killian didn't deserve my tears.

I barely slept, and when I woke up, I was in a bad mood, which only put a bigger wrench between Evelyn and me. Evelyn didn't even hide her glare when Fabula summoned me.

The next three days went by like the first one—I trained with Fabula most of the day. Cyrene joined us a few times, helping with some spells. We had lunch in her throne room, and when we needed a break, we sat down and talked. Fabula told me more and more about my mother. About how bright and impossible and loyal she had been. About how she once stuck her neck out for a new witch who was floundering, but with my mother's guidance, had grown into a great witch. About how my mother had found a stray cat and tried convincing Fabula's mother that it was her familiar, so she could keep the poor kitty. About how they had almost burned down the room when practicing spells that required fire—though no light or dark witch could yield fire. It burned not only flesh, but also our magic.

I thought I would never get tired of hearing stories about my mother.

Heath also joined us several times—sometimes as a Dark Order member, sometimes as Fabula's son. He paid attention to me, helped me out during spells, pulled my chair back when I sat down at the table, opened doors for me, and plain stared at me with interest.

I didn't want to admit it, but I desperately wanted the attention.

The first night after I went to see Killian, Evelyn didn't come to me and I didn't go to her. I didn't know if Killian had told Asher what had happened—I doubted it—and Asher had told her, and now the gap between us was wider. Though, even if she didn't know about Killian and me, she could see what was happening at the coven. Fabula favored me, and Evelyn didn't seem to be the only jealous witch around.

During one of my short breaks, I went to the kitchen to get tea. Fabula wanted the human servants to bring it to me, but I needed to stretch my legs. And, on my way there, I overheard Peony and another witch talking about Fabula being blinded by me. She had forgone all of her other duties to spend time with me, to train me personally, something that hadn't happened before.

I thought that would make me feel ashamed, but it was quite the opposite. I liked Fabula's attention. And what if she favored me? It would serve me well if I stayed.

Especially if I helped Evelyn find and steal the box, and then stayed here, as if I had done nothing.

On my fifth afternoon training with Fabula, I could feel Evelyn's potion wearing off. I was tired and missing more than usual, and the spells didn't come as I wanted them too. The sparks and bolts started fading.

After calling for sweet tea and pastries, Fabula suggested I take the rest of the day off.

"No, I'm fine," I told her. Even though this magic was borrowed, I was learning so much. I wanted to keep practicing.

"I have an idea," Heath said, stepping closer. Today, he was here as a Dark Order member, with the black leather uniform and the sword at his waist. "I could take Lavinia for a stroll. Take her mind off training for a while. That might help."

Fabula's eyes lit up. "That's a wonderful idea."

Fabula practically pushed Heath and me out of the door.

Once outside the throne room, I turned to him. "You don't need to do this."

He held my gaze. "I want to."

He guided me to a sitting room with leather couches and low tables, and a glass wall that opened to a balcony—like ten other rooms in the lodge. But this balcony had a narrow stone path to the side that wound up the mountain.

Heath grabbed thick cloaks from a hidden closet in the room and offered one to me. I wrapped it around me before exiting to the balcony.

I stepped onto the stone path, wary. "How come it's not covered by the snow?"

"It's enchanted," he said.

Of course it was.

Trees flanked the path as we walked. "You were on duty. Shouldn't you be back at the lodge?"

"I'm the captain," he said, trailing beside me. "I called in another guard to take my place." The path forked in two, and Heath gestured to the one to the right. "This way."

We followed the path up the mountain. The slope was slight, but after training, fatigue clung to my bones. "Are we going somewhere specific?"

He offered me a wolfish grin. "You'll see."

A moment later, the path widened and curved around itself, making a wide circle along thin trees—icicles covered the branches, which glittered in the bright sunlight, creating rainbows across the pristine snow-scape.

I gasped. "It's incredible."

"I knew you would like it."

I turned to Heath, placing a hand on his arm. "Thank you for bringing me here," I said, my voice low.

"I have heard many stories about your mother growing up. My mother misses her a lot." He reached over and took my hand in his. I froze, and it wasn't because of the cold. "But now you're here and I haven't seen my mother this happy in a long time."

"I'm happy too." It wasn't a lie. Even if I wasn't happy about everything, I felt content about learning more about my mother.

I looked down at our joined hands; my traitorous heart squeezed. I wished I was holding Killian's hand instead, but that was an empty wish. If I stayed, there would be no Killian.

But there would be Heath.

I met his unyielding gaze. He was handsome, a badass warrior, and so far he had been respectful and kind. He looked at me in a way that made me feel seen. Desired.

Perhaps it would take time for me to push Killian out of

my heart, but I could see it happening, especially if Heath was patient with me.

Heath brought my hand up, kissing the top, his gaze holding mine. Warmth spread through my cheeks. "I have to tell you, ever since I first saw you, it has been hard to take my eyes off you."

The warmth turned into heat. I wasn't used to the attention but I kind of liked it.

His eyes landed on my lips and he leaned into me.

I snapped out of it. I pulled my hand from his and stepped back.

"Forgi—"

"No," I croaked. I cleared my throat. "It's okay. It's my fault."

He tilted his head. "Out of a recent relationship?"

Shit. "Something like that."

He nodded. "I understand." He showed me a small grin. "I'm patient."

I sighed in relief.

After that, we stayed in the icicle garden for a few more minutes and then he escorted me back to the lodge. He took me to the kitchen, where he made hot cocoa for me.

I felt so bad because so far, my heart wasn't it, but I knew, I just knew it could be. In time, it could be.

On the fourth night after my visit to the inn, Evelyn finally came to my bedroom.

She crossed her arms and frowned at me. "You've given up, haven't you? What will you do? Turn me in to Fabula?"

I shook my head. "I would never. Besides ... I haven't given up." It was true. As much as I fantasized about staying here and making a life for myself, it wasn't easy to make the leap.

I also worried a little when Fabula found out about the blood promise. She would know I lied to her about my magic, that I took potions to enhance it so I could trick her ... she wouldn't take it well.

Unless I told her I had been trying to impress her, not trick her. That I wanted to join the coven so bad, I had been willing to do anything.

She might buy that.

"Then why haven't we found your damn box yet and left this place?" she asked, annoyed. "Is it because of Heath?"

I gaped at her.

"Don't pretend it's not obvious. Everyone in this damn lodge has noticed he has been fawning over you since we arrived."

"What if he is? What's so bad about that?"

Her eyes narrowed. "I thought you liked Killian."

I frowned. "Unrequited love doesn't really work for me."

She shook her head at me. "What happened to you? Are you really buying all the shit they are selling you? You can't be serious!"

"It isn't shit!" I yelled. "My mother was a Nightmist witch. They proved it to me."

Her mouth fell open. "Wow, you're sinking fast and deep. And here I thought we could be great friends. You're choosing dark witches over me. Over Killian. So, you have no interest in the box anymore?"

The box be damned! "If you're so eager to go, then take your dragon teeth and leave!"

Evelyn winced. "Wow, what has Fabula done to you? She really has you trapped in her web."

I clenched my fists and teeth, and it was all I could not to yell at her. I inhaled deeply and let the tension go. Killian,

Evelyn ... they would never understand what it was to meet someone who knew your mother inside and out, and was more than willing to share. Who welcomed you like family. Who treated you like a best friend.

Evelyn had found Asher, but it wasn't the same thing. He was her home.

This, here, was mine.

I gasped with the realization.

"Forget about it," she snapped. "I'll do this myself."

She marched out of my bedroom and slammed the door behind her.

I stared at the door for a minute, shocked by my feelings. But as the seconds ticked by, I felt surer and surer. This was the right thing.

Tomorrow night, I would help Evelyn take the box and the dragon bones and escape. Then, I would come up with an excuse about her using me to get to them, then knocking me out or whatever—I had the entire day tomorrow to figure out what to do.

Later, I slipped into bed with my chest full.

This was it. I was staying. I had finally found where I belonged.

16

———

IT TURNED OUT THE NEXT MORNING, THE LODGE WAS ABUZZ with activity.

"What's going on?" I asked Lorie and Keeva during breakfast.

"Tonight is the full moon," Lorie said with a singsong tone.

I frowned.

Keeva rolled her eyes. "She doesn't know, Lorie." She looked at me as if she was a teacher and I was a child. "Every full moon, we celebrate outside. It's a big deal. You'll love it."

A big party under the full moon every month? It sounded heavenly. One more great point for my decision to stay.

Because of the preparations, I didn't have my usual practice with Fabula, but I got to help out with enchanted flower arrangements to be placed outside. I barely saw Evelyn all day, and I was really dreading it. I wanted to tell her about my decision, and at the same time, I didn't. I would break the news after the party. Hopefully, the witches would be all drunk and having sex with their beloved humans, and they wouldn't see us sneaking around the lodge.

If Fabula and the other witches cornered me after Evelyn left with the items, I would tell them that Evelyn had used me to help her sneak into the lodge. She probably knew my mother was a Nightmist witch, and everyone would be so busy wrapping their heads around that, we wouldn't even see her true purpose for coming here. I would act betrayed—sad and enraged. I hoped they bought it, because otherwise my plan would fail. And I didn't want to think what the witches would do to me then.

At sunset, we all changed into long black robes with cinched waists, the wide sleeves covering our fingers and the hoods dipping lower to conceal our eyes, and met at the front of the lodge. It had been magically cleared of snow and warmed up because of the cold, and now had many colorful rugs, pillows, tables, tents made of thin black fabric, the flowers arrangements I had helped with, and tiki-styles torches spread around the perimeter. In a corner, an enchanted violin and piano played, filling the air with a low, melodious tune.

The witches lounged on the pillows, forming little groups on the rugs, and the human servants came around, bringing trays of food and drinks and placing them among the witches. Lorie, Keeva, and Dot sat with me and a handful of other witches whose names I didn't remember. Evelyn sat in a distant corner, practically by herself.

At the center of the party, a silver pedestal was placed with an elaborated golden chalice on top. I wondered what that meant, but once some witches got up and started dancing and laughing, I forgot all about it.

Soon, the Dark Order escorted Fabula and Cyrene.

Fabula walked among the witches and smiled at all of us. "It's the full moon, my darlings!"

The witches cheered.

She raised her arms high. "Our most beloved night of every month." The shouts became louder. "This will be a night to remember."

She snapped her fingers and the music grew louder and faster, and all of the witches jumped up and began dancing. Drinks flowed faster, the food was gone, and as the sky darkened, the party got louder and louder. The male humans I had seen at the nightclub and my first party here weaved through the witches, dancing among them—and the witches couldn't take their hands off them.

The feel of the party was heavy and contagious. I couldn't help it. I drank a glass of wine and let that small buzz carry me away. I danced with my sisters, and when Lorie and Keeva playfully sandwiched me and rubbed their bodies against mine, I laughed.

Fabula and Cyrene made the rounds, stopping by each little group, dancing and chatting and laughing with all of the witches—always followed by a couple of Dark Order guards. When she stopped by our group, she hugged me tight.

"I'm so happy you're here, my darling."

"Me too." I held on to her.

Not long after that, she moved on to another group, and I continued dancing with Lorie, Keeva, and Dot.

The sky was dark and the full moon was on beautiful display amid the stars when I finally took a breather. Sweaty, but feeling freer than ever, I walked to the corner of the arranged area, where a tray with drinks had recently been left. I picked up another glass of wine and sipped from it. I probably shouldn't be drinking if I was going to help Evelyn escape later tonight, but right now, I didn't care. I was having fun and feeling at home for once in my life.

"I see you're enjoying the party," Heath said from behind me.

I glanced over my shoulder and found him standing there, a few feet to my five, very cool and neat in the Dark Order's uniform. I took another sip from my drink and turned to him. "I am," I said with a smile. Right now, the buzz in my veins told me Heath looked sexy and dangerous. I cocked my eyebrows at him. "It's a shame you're on duty. Otherwise, I would ask you to dance."

Without missing a beat, Heath stepped closer, wrapped his arm around my waist, and pulled me flush against him. "I'm the captain. I can do whatever I want." He leaned into me and whispered, "And I want to dance with you."

Heath looked over my head and nodded slightly. I followed his line of sight—another Dark Order member, who responded with the same nod.

"Was that you telling him you're taking a break?" I asked.

"Exactly." His arm tightened around my waist and then we were spinning around, weaving around the witches, the human males, and the human servants who stood at attention to bring more food or drinks if needed.

Heath guided me expertly through the crowd, dodging the unruly witches who jumped and danced without rhyme or reason. When we passed Fabula, she smiled affectionately at us.

"I think she's rooting for us," Heath said.

I nodded. "I think so too."

He looked into my eyes. "Can I root for us too?"

I bit the inside of my cheek. Could he? I stared at him, at

his dark eyes and handsome face. And, without warning, his face was replaced with Killian's in my head—the hot and moody vampire. I shouldn't think of him. I shouldn't see him in another guy. Yet, there wasn't much I could do about that.

I forced Killian's image from my mind, focusing on the guy who gave me his attention, who didn't seem ashamed of it. If I stayed, I bet I could fall for Heath. I bet it wouldn't be difficult.

"Perhaps," I finally said.

That earned me a half-smile.

As I suspected, the witches didn't just dance with the human males—some had them on the floor, where they rode the men. In a corner, a witch had her robes up to her waist and she was being sandwiched by two males, who moved in the same fast rhythm. A little to the side, a witch was on her knees in front of a male, his pants down to his thighs, his hands in her hair, his eyes closed and his lips parted.

My body grew hot and I tried not watching, not hearing it.

"Here." Heath moved us to the center of the area, where no one was having sex. "This is better."

I frowned, wondering if he didn't like seeing that either. I mean, sex was great. I hadn't had any since I broke up with Adrian, but it had been really good back then. But I certainly didn't want to watch others doing it.

At eleven, the music lowered to a faint whisper and the witches stopped.

Heath leaned into me and said, "The big show is about to start. Stay here." He retreated to the perimeter, where he joined the other Dark Order members.

Curiosity welled in me, but I stayed put.

Fabula and Cyrene came forward and stood beside the pedestal and the chalice.

"It's time, my darlings," Fabula said. The witches screamed in delight.

Fabula gestured for someone to come over. Five human servants dressed in simple white clothing walked from among the crowd and stood in front of her, all of them females.

Cyrene handed a dagger to Fabula. Without ceremony, Fabula slashed her palm with it. I gasped, but no one seemed surprised by it.

"Honor this night," Fabula said. She clenched her hand and the blood dropped to the ground. "Honor this place." She started walking around the humans and the pedestal. "Honor this sky." The trickle of blood didn't stop, and I thought that if she kept losing blood like that, she would faint. "Honor this sisterhood." She closed the blood circle. "Honor this moon." She rose both arms above her head.

All the witches did the same. Even the Dark Order copied her move. Lost, I too lifted my arms.

Evelyn, watching everything with hawk eyes from the edge of the rugs, crossed her arms defiantly. If someone noticed, no one said a word about it.

Then, Fabula swiped the dagger wide.

And slit a human's throat. I jerked back in horror as blood oozed down her neck, soaking her white clothes. Trembling, the human fell to her knees, then face-first at Fabula's feet.

Around me, the witches cheered.

What the hell was going on?

Fabula moved to the next human and stabbed the dagger into her heart. She pulled the dagger back. Another body down.

She went on—killing the other three humans in the most gruesome and bloody manner, while they stood there, waiting for their turn. They had to be drugged or enchanted. How come they were not yelling, running, desperate?

Fabula smiled wide when the last body hit the floor, and the witches' screams turned deafening.

I pressed a hand to my stomach as it revolved with horror and disgust.

But it wasn't over. Fabula handed the dagger back to Cyrene and picked up the chalice. She knelt down and placed the chalice under the bleeding wounds, filling it with blood.

Holding the chalice high, she stood.

She drank from the chalice.

My dinner came back up, but I was able to hold it in.

Oh my God ...

"Rejoice, sisters!" Fabula shouted loudest of all. "We're honoring the moon." She passed on the chalice to Cyrene, who drank a sip. Then Cyrene passed on to Lorie, who also drank from the chalice. Lorie gave the chalice to Dot and she too drank the blood.

I was getting more and more nauseous by the second.

Desperation filled my pores. Did they expect all the witches here to drink from the chalice?

Perhaps this shouldn't shock me so much. After all, I was half in love with a vampire who drank blood, but as far as I knew, he drank animal blood. Not humans'.

The only exception to that had been when he drank from my parents' and his brother's killers. I hadn't really minded then.

Besides, as a vampire, he couldn't help it. Blood was his food.

Now ... these witches didn't need blood. They didn't have to do this.

Killing these humans and drinking their blood was plain wrong and evil.

My eyes met Evelyn's from across the mad crowd. She had a deep frown, and her jaw was tight to match Killian's. She nodded her head toward the lodge, an almost imperceptible gesture.

Afraid someone could see me, I blinked both eyes slowly.

Slowly, I retreated to the edge of the party area.

Heath appeared by my side and I froze in place. "Such a display of power," he said, clearly enchanted by the scene. He glanced at me, at my probably pale face. "Don't worry, they won't make you drink on your first night. Unless you want to. My mother would love it, actually."

My eyes widened. "Do they do this every full moon?"

He nodded. "Yes. It's an honoring sacrifice to the moon and its power."

The moon's power was believed to be linked to all supernaturals. Though I doubted the moon wanted this kind of blood on her hands.

"Well, I would rather go slow," I said, my voice faint.

He nodded. "I thought so. Just stay here. I'll take care of it."

I held still and barely breathed as the minutes ticked by. The chalice went around, approaching my place inch by inch. I wanted to run away, but with Heath right beside me, I couldn't. He would tell his mother I had fled after this savage display.

They would see through me.

They would know I had changed my mind.

I didn't care if this was my mother's coven. That she had

grown up among these witches, that she had participated in these insane rituals. It didn't matter when it went against my morals.

Tonight, I wasn't only helping Evelyn escape.

I would escape with her.

17

The party went on longer than I hoped.

When the chalice came my way, Heath deflected it, and no one said a word about it. After all of them drank a little of the humans' blood, the music became louder once more and the dancing and drinking resumed—and the bodies stayed there, strewn on the rugs, blood pooling around them.

Some witches even soaked their feet in blood.

Holy shit, I couldn't take this anymore.

I yawned, pretending to be exhausted and dizzy, and made my way to my bedroom. Heath started escorting me.

"Don't be silly," I told him with a fake small smile. "Stay. Enjoy the party."

"Are you sure?"

Yes, I was sure. I wanted him and all the witches far away from me.

Once in my bedroom, I changed out of those robes and into my leggings, sweater, and boots. My hands shook as I slipped my dagger inside my boots, got my jacket, along with my bag and all of my things. If I forgot something, that was okay. I didn't want anything that reminded me of this place.

I halted in front of the mirror and looked into my eyes—eyes that were supposed to be like my mother's.

This had been her family, her home.

But it wasn't mine. Not like this.

I had to believe my mother was better than this. That she had left because she too couldn't take the savage sacrifices, the evilness in their ways.

Shit, I had been wrong. So, so blind.

I inhaled deeply. I could stay here and cry and lament my stupidity, or I could do something about it.

In the dead of night, I tiptoed to Evelyn's room. I knocked softly on the door, and not even five seconds later, she opened a small crack. When she saw it was me, she opened it wide and urged me in.

I entered her room and she shut the door. A lamp was on beside her bed, and I could see she had the same plan as me—her bag was ready on the bed and she had her black pants on, black sweater and vest, and thick boots.

Evelyn crossed her arms. "I thought you were staying."

"Me too, but ..." I sighed. "You saw what they did tonight. I don't want any part of that."

"What about your mother? Wasn't this her coven?"

"If it really was, then she knew this was wrong and that's why she left."

She watched me for a tense minute, until finally she dropped her arms and relaxed. "I'm glad you aren't *that* stupid."

I rolled my eyes at her. "Yeah. Yeah. Now, let's go. The witches are either drunk, or having sex, or passed out, so now is our opportunity."

Evelyn nodded. "I texted Asher earlier. He knows I'll be leaving tonight."

I frowned. "What about Killian?"

She shrugged. "He didn't say anything about Killian."

My stomach tensed with apprehension. Killian could have heeded my words and left. Or he could be waiting for Evelyn to get out with the box before he continued his journey to DuMoir Castle. Either way, I shouldn't hope he had stayed because of me.

But I couldn't help myself.

Evelyn grabbed her bag, and we slipped out of her bedroom. The first and second hallways we took were deserted, but we encountered the tiger in the third one. Evelyn handed me two potions—invisibility and cloaking. She drank both, so I did the same. I wrinkled my nose at the tart taste of the second one, but I felt it acting right away. Magic enveloped me and I turned invisible, and my scent was cloaked. The tiger wouldn't be able to sniff us.

Holding our breath, Evelyn and I waited by a corner until the tiger strolled by, as if he had nothing better to do than take his time with each one of his steps.

Once he was several feet away, we continued down the hallway.

I couldn't see Evelyn either, but she had a firm grasp on my hand and didn't let go.

At the stairs, we saw two Dark Order members. For a few more minutes, the invisibility potion would still work, so we tiptoed around them.

Even though we moved slowly and silently, the tension was so heavy, by the time we arrived on the first floor, I felt as if we had run a marathon.

The raven perched beside the fireplace at the lobby, but it

had its beak down. I thought it was sleeping. Either way, it couldn't see us. In the dim lighting, we took the corridor toward the metal door and heard voices. Like we had done before, we plastered ourselves to a doorway and remained as still as we could.

"... wasn't so bad," a female said.

"She always seems strong during the full moon sacrifices," a second female voice said.

Despite myself, I leaned closer to where the voices were coming from, and before I knew it, I was spying through the small crack of a door. It was Hester and Peony, seated on a couch in a room with low lighting, speaking in soft tones.

"But then she's not," Hester said. "We need to do something."

I frowned. What the hell was this about? Was it them I had heard? They seemed to be plotting against Fabula.

Well, not my problem anymore.

By the time they did something—*if* they did something—I would be long gone.

Evelyn tugged on my hand. Right. We had to go. She pulled us through the corridor, and we stopped in front of the metal door. She let go of my hand, and from the faint sound, she was using the same method as before to open it. The click sounded and the door opened, by itself—or rather, Evelyn pushed it. Her hand slapped me as she tried to find me. I helped her, and then we were moving again.

We stepped into the dark room and I stopped short, my breath caught.

Right there, on the long table, was the box. The moonlight coming from the window illuminated it like a spotlight.

"Is this the box?" Evelyn asked in a low voice.

I nodded. Realizing she couldn't see me, I said, "Yes."

It was like Killian's box—right now, it looked like a rectangular black stone with smooth surfaces, no bigger than my forearm.

The Nightmist witches really had found a box. The pull, the call I felt had been right.

"Stay here," Evelyn said. "I'll get the dragon teeth and then we have to go. We have ... two minutes before the potion wears off."

She let go of my hand. Springing into action, I fished a shirt from my bag and reached for the box.

Bright light inundated the room and I squinted against it. My heart hammered against my chest. What the hell was going on? Slowly, the light dimmed until only a few lamps around the room shone.

From across the table, Evelyn stared at me, her eyes wide.

"I can see you," I said, stunned. Shouldn't the potion work for another minute and some seconds?

"What's going on?" she asked me.

Shadows emerged from between the bookshelves.

Princess Fabula, followed closely by Cyrene, Heath, and Tade.

I inhaled deeply.

Fabula showed me a vicious smile. "My darling, did you think I didn't know?"

18

I stared at Fabula, completely shocked. What did she mean? She knew what exactly?

Before I could ask anything, Cyrene snapped her fingers and the other seven members of the Dark Order entered the room, along with Lorie, Keeva, Dot, and a handful of other witches. The tiger also appeared by the door, and the raven flew in and took a spot on a bookshelf.

My muscles tensed. Shit, we were surrounded.

Slowly, Evelyn backed up until she stood by my side.

Fabula halted across the table, right behind the box. "I have a little confession to make." She looked at me. "I've never met your mother and she certainly wasn't a Nightmist witch."

The blood rushed from my face. "W-what?" I glanced around at all the witches standing them. All of them had said they met my mother, that they missed her. "But ... you told me about her."

Fabula shrugged. "I only told you what you wanted to hear, my darling."

My head spun. "How?"

"Ah, see, every light and dark witch has a special gift." She pointed to Cyrene, standing a few feet from him. "Cyrene here can see links between magic and history. As for me ..." She raised her hands, palms turned to me, and wiggled her fingers. "Mine is to touch and see."

I frowned. So, when Evelyn and I first met Cyrene, she must have seen ... what? My connection to the box and Evelyn's to the dragon teeth? And when Fabula first touched me at our first dinner here, she saw ... "What did you see?" I asked, my voice turning harsh.

"I see random images, but I'm over one hundred and fifty years old, my darling. After so long, I've learned to make educated guesses, and ninety-nine percent of the time, I'm right. With you, I saw your mother, I saw your claustrophobia, and learned a little about your parents' death. I saw how you desperately wanted a place to belong, and I saw the blood promise."

I could barely breathe. Here she was, confessing she had lied to me. She had played with me, used my emotions to trick me. All of them had been on it.

I glanced at Heath and he watched me, his eyes colder than Killian's had ever been.

"You were playing with me," I whispered.

"If you hadn't come to steal the stone, if you had bought our lie and just stayed like a good witch, then maybe it could have been more than that," he said, no emotion on his face or voice.

I pressed a hand to my chest, my knees weakened. I had been so completely duped.

So completely stupid.

"I wouldn't have minded that," Fabula said. "You would

have made a good pair for him. If you had behaved and done what we had hoped you would."

"You want a clay doll to mold," Evelyn snapped.

Cyrene glared at her. "Stay quiet. This doesn't concern you. We're only tolerating you here because of her." She pointed at me.

Wait, so, they still cared for me? No, there had to be more to it.

Fabula placed a finger on the box's smooth surface. "As I was saying before, I saw things when I touched you ... and I saw this stone." The fact that she had called it a stone, like those demons, didn't escape me. "When you came to the nightclub, Cyrene saw your connection to it right away. And then it was confirmed when I saw you holding a stone like this one."

Before I could hold my tongue, I asked, "How did you find it?"

Fabula smiled at me, but she didn't answer.

Lorie did. "I can see magical items when I'm near them. I saw the stone and we went after it. We found it buried deep in a cave in this mountain."

Fabula looked at her. "When was it? About three weeks ago?"

Lorie nodded. "It was like the stone and its power woke up from a long slumber."

I frowned and did the math in my head. That was when I first touched Killian's box.

Fabula drew her finger along the box's corners. "I can feel its power, but I don't know how it works, what its purpose is, and more importantly, why such an object was hidden." Her finger froze. "But you do. You know."

I clenched my jaw. So she hadn't seen me opening the

box with my touch. She didn't see Killian coming out of it, and she certainly didn't see me using its power to defeat the demon hunters. Good.

Now, if she thought I would tell her anything, she was sorely mistaken. She tilted her head. "But you won't tell me, will you? Not so easily. It's okay. We have time. " She let out a sigh. "Take them."

The Dark Order tightened the circle around us, their hands on their swords. The tiger stalked closer, snarling. Cyrene, Lorie, Keeva, Dot, and the other witches advanced on us. They grabbed for us, and Evelyn and I fought back. But Keeva zapped me with a dark jolt that came from her fingertips. It hit me in the neck and everything went dark.

I DIDN'T KNOW if the splitting headache had woken me, or if it started hurting once I came to, but as I sat up on the cold, rough floor, I groaned in pain. I blinked, trying to get through the pain. Finally, I opened my eyes.

My breath seized. I was seated on the uneven, dirty ground of a three-by-three cell with gray stone walls and metal bars on one side, and no windows. The light here was low, constantly flickering as if there was a torch in the hallway outside and a draft threatened to extinguish it at any moment.

The scent of mold and rust was heavy, and despite how damn cold it was in here, my skin felt sticky.

I looked down at myself and found thin metal bracelets around my wrists. What the ...?

I crawled to the bars and looked out. Across the hallway, there were more cells. I couldn't see Evelyn, but two cells to the left, someone curled in a corner. From the shoulder's span and foot's size, it could only be a male. A human servant who misbehaved? I didn't care about that now.

"Evelyn?" I called. A groan answered me, and it seemed to be coming from the cell to my left. "Is that you?"

I heard shuffling and then her voice. "Yes." She groaned again. "Ow, my head."

"Mine too. It's probably whatever they gave us," I said.

"I have some kind of bracelet," she said. "I think ... Yeah, I tried to zap the lock and it didn't work."

I glanced down at the metal cuffs. "I have them too. They're probably inhibiting our magic."

"Damn it." She sighed. "I'm sorry."

I frowned. "About?"

"About your mother," she said, her voice low. "About it all being a trick."

"Me too," I whispered. A black hole formed in my chest. Fabula had created an intricate lie, and enrolled all of the witches and the Dark Order members in her ridiculous tale. She had gone through all of that trouble to hold me here.

Because of the damn box.

"Do you want—?"

I cut her off. "Let's just forget about that." I had to because I couldn't deal with my emotions right now. I needed to focus on a plan. "We need to find a way out of here."

The figure in the cell across the hallway moved. The male turned to us, and still lying on the floor, he stared at us. He too had the thin metal cuffs on his wrists.

"There's no way out," he said, his voice rough as if it hadn't been used in a while. For a moment, he reminded me of Killian when he had come out of the box—unruly and longish hair, an uneven beard, and ragged pants and shirt.

But this guy had a light-olive skin and dark eyes. "If there was, I wouldn't be here."

"Who are you?" Evelyn asked.

"Just ... someone." He turned his back to us again.

"Ignore him," I said, wary. "We *need* to get out here."

"Agreed, but—"

Footsteps echoed down the hallway—the heavy stomp of boots.

I scooted to the back of my cell, suddenly scared. After all, I was weak and in a cell, surrounded by hundreds of powerful witches. This wasn't going very well for me.

Heath, Deron, and Tade appeared in front of our cells, but I could see the shadows of the other Dark Order members close by.

"Get up," Heath said. A veil had fallen over him since Fabula revealed their trick. It was like he had never smiled at me, looked at me with interest. Like he had never tried to kiss me.

I didn't move.

Heath lifted his hand, revealing two large bronze keys in his hand. He held them together and turned them. Magic jolted through my wrists, shaking my core and robbing me of air.

In the cell beside mine, Evelyn gasped.

"Get up before I do it again," Heath said.

The pain lingered, but I pushed to my feet. Heath separated the keys and turned one. Evelyn cried out.

"Get up, Evelyn," I said, my voice breaking. We couldn't win right now, but if she didn't move, if she didn't do what they wanted, we wouldn't be able to win later. "Please."

The shuffling of feet reached my ears.

Heath pocketed the keys. Tade went to Evelyn's cell and

Deron stepped closer to mine. He unlocked the barred door of my cell and opened it wide.

"Out," Heath said.

I walked to the door. Before I could exit, Deron stopped in front of me and grabbed my wrists. He placed a metal bar between the cuffs that magically attached itself to them, creating a link and locking my wrists together.

"Try anything funny and I'll enjoy hurting you," he said with a hiss.

He meant it, I knew that; I barely dared to breathe.

"Go," Heath said, pointing to the doorway at the end of the hallway, where the six Dark Order soldiers remained.

With Evelyn by my side, I walked forward. That was when I realized I must have fallen and hit my shoulder and hips when I fainted, or when I was thrown into the cell, because my right side hurt like hell, especially when I moved.

When we reached the Dark Order, they closed around us, forming a living corridor that escorted us past the doorway, up a set of stone stairs, down another crude hallway, and into a sitting room in the lodge. I frowned, wondering if the lodge had always had a dungeon underneath it, or if the witches had carved it out of the mountain after they settled here.

The Dark Order brought us to the lobby, where Fabula and Cyrene waited for us, seated on two chaise lounges in front of the fireplace. Besides them, at least a quarter of the witches who lived here were spread out through the space. They laughed and cheered and catcalled us as we walked by.

Outside, the sun rose behind the mountain in a beautiful display of red and orange. It was almost an insult.

When we were in the center of the room, Heath lifted his closed hand and everyone stopped.

Fabula got up from her chaise. "Oh, there you are. Come on." She beckoned us closer. "You don't want to miss it."

I glanced at Evelyn, and she shook her head slightly. Heath picked up the keys.

I stepped forward. "All right. We're going."

Fabula strolled to the glass wall and halted in front of it. Evelyn and I stopped beside her. Then Fabula smiled at Heath. "We're ready." She turned her eyes to us. "Let the show begin."

I frowned. What the hell was she talking about?

Heath and the other Dark Order members exited the lobby through one of the glass doors. They rushed down the balcony stairs and went to the snow-covered lodge entrance.

A moment later, the dark zaps of magic flew from the trees surrounding the area. Then a witch flew past the trees and skidded over the snow. She fell face-first; a red pool quickly formed around her.

I gasped in horror.

Killian and Asher stomped out from the trees—Killian with the dark lines around his eyes, and Asher with a large sword in his hands. My heart stopped.

A dozen witches attacked them and the Dark Order ran toward them.

"No," I whispered.

Beside me, Fabula laughed. "Isn't this a spectacle? It's going to be incredible!"

I couldn't tear my gaze from Killian and Asher as they plowed through the witches. Asher threw potions at the two incoming soldiers and green smoke filled the air around him. A moment later, the two soldiers and the two closest witches were down in the snow.

Killian was a blur of movement. He ran from one soldier

to the other, and from witch to witch, an invisible force breaking necks and ripping throats out.

Another dozen witches came from the side of the mountain, and Killian and Asher plowed through them in the same way.

Serious now, Fabula looked over at Cyrene. She nodded and walked past the glass doors, followed by Lorie, Keeva, Dot, Hester, Peony, and a handful of other witches. Meanwhile, two dozen witches surged from under the lodge and surrounded Killian and Asher.

A dark line flashed around them, a large witch's circle.

No.

Killian and Asher stopped. They gritted their teeth and jerked against the force immobilizing them. But they were two fighting against many powerful witches.

They couldn't win.

Killian fell to his knees. Asher followed.

Heath and Tade stepped into the circle and snapped metal cuffs around Killian's and Asher's wrists—the same cuffs Evelyn and I wore.

Now, they couldn't fight back.

Heath fished something out of his pocket. A flash of silver shone under the sunlight. A syringe. Heath pressed it against Killian's shoulder. A moment later, Killian's body folded in the snow.

"No!" I cried, banging my hands on the glass wall.

Fabula reached over and touched the link connecting my cuffs. A dark electric jolt zapped from her finger, and I cried as it rattled my bones. My knees jerked and locked, and I leaned against the glass wall.

My breathing shallowed, my vision darkened.

"Take her," Fabula said to someone. "Take them all."

19

I THOUGHT I WAS GOING TO PASS OUT AGAIN, BUT I DIDN'T. I held on to clarity and strength and remained conscious as a handful of witches took Evelyn and me back to the dungeons.

Moments later, the Dark Order came in carrying a fighting Asher and a mostly unconscious Killian. They threw the guys in separate cells across from ours, locked the doors, and then left.

Asher wrapped his hand around the bars. "Evie, are you okay?"

"Yes," she said from my right. If I strained against the bars, I could see her arm jutting through, trying to reach Asher on the other side. The corridor was too wide for that. "How about you?"

They kept talking, but I tuned them out. Instead, I sat along the bars and watched Killian. He had fallen where they left him and hadn't moved since. It had been a few minutes, but as the seconds ticked by, my anxiety increased. Why wasn't he moving? Why wasn't he waking up?

He launched to his feet, turning.

I sucked in a breath.

The black lines veined his dark eyes, and his fangs were out. He snarled at the bars, ramming them with all of his strength, which between the sedative and the cuffs around his wrists wasn't much. Breathing hard, he fell on his knees.

Then, he shot up and tried it again. He rammed the bars, punched the stone walls, wrapped his hands around the bars and tried breaking them, kicked the door, but other than rattling everything and hurting himself more, nothing happened.

I knew what he was going through because I had had this before too. When the demon hunters locked me in the closet with Killian, I had panicked. Like, really panicked because I had relived my worst nightmare.

This was Killian's—being drugged and trapped in a dungeon in a place full of witches ... though the first time it had been by warlocks. Killian was reliving the time he had been put in the box.

My eyes filled with tears. "Killian," I whispered.

His dark eyes met mine.

Slowly, the black lines disappeared and the fangs retreated. "Lavinia," he said, his voice broken. Hurt. He crouched beside the bars.

I fought against the tears that threatened to spill at any moment. "What are you doing here? I told you to go."

"Did you really think I could leave you?" He stared at me, his gaze unflinching. "That would be the same as ripping my dead heart out."

I swallowed a sob.

"For the moon's sake, you're all damn loud," the man in the cell beside Killian's said. He turned around again and faced me, then Evelyn. "I've been here for months now, and it's been peace and quiet. You all got here a few hours ago, and it has been hell ever since."

"Who the hell are you?" Asher asked, trying to look through the bars.

"You've been here for months?" Evelyn asked at the same time. "Why?"

He sat up, folding his long legs in front of him. "Let's say the witches here were paid to help a wolf shifter in my pack kill my father and take over as alpha." He paused. "I was supposed to be killed too, but the witches decided to have fun with me instead."

"You mean ... they torture you?" I asked, my voice low.

"No, sweetheart, it's because I'm too handsome." His voice was full of sarcasm. "Yeah. They used to torture me, in the beginning." He grew serious as he opened his arms, and even from here, I could see the scars covering his skin, along with large tribal-like tattoos. "But I think they've been busy with something else the last few weeks, because they have left me alone. There are days they don't even feed me."

"So you're a werewolf?" Killian asked, his voice strained. I could see he was still struggling with all of this. Perhaps talking about someone else's problem helped.

"My pack prefers the term wolf shifter," the guy said. "But yeah, basically, I'm a werewolf. I'm Shane."

We introduced ourselves to him, telling him what we were and a brief version of why we were here.

What a group we were. A wolf shifter, a human, a witch, a vampire, and a half witch and half demon hunter. And yet, here we were. Locked in this dungeon without a way of escaping.

"I can't accept that this is it," Evelyn said. "There has to be a way out of here. We just need to think."

"Do you see the cuffs around your wrists, sweetheart?" Shane's sarcasm was back. "With those, I can't shift, you can't do any spell, and I bet the vamp here can't turn either."

"He can," I said, looking at Killian. When he was first brought in, he had his vampire-mode on. But the cuffs had just been put on him. "Right?"

Killian stood and turned his back to me. A few seconds later, he turned back. "I can, but I can't hold it for long."

Shit.

"See, sweetheart?" Shane cocked an eyebrow at me. "There's nothing we can do now."

Killian paced in his cell, Asher leaned against the bars, and Shane sat with his back against the stone wall.

I looked around my cell, as if I could find something hidden there. A hole, a secret door, a key ... something. I hadn't come all this way to give up and be trapped in a damn cold and dirty cell.

But as the seconds turned into minutes, and then into hours, and nothing happened, no one produced an idea, we didn't find anything, I became doubtful.

Without my phone and a window to see the sky, there was no way to tell time. At some point, I must have napped on the floor, because I woke up with a start when footsteps echoed in the hallway.

I sat up straighter. From where I could see, Killian and Asher stood at attention too, not too close to the bars. The only one who didn't seem to care was Shane. He stayed seated along the back wall, his eyes closed.

Fabula, Cyrene, and Heath came into view, but I could

hear the sound of more people at the dungeon's doorway. They halted between my cell and Killian's. Fabula looked at me. She snapped her fingers and Heath stepped forward. He offered me a glass with water.

I narrowed my eyes at the glass. Was this another trick?

With a sigh, Heath took the glass to his lips and drank a big gulp. "It's not poisoned. If we wanted to kill you, you would be dead already."

I glanced at Shane. No, they didn't like to kill. They liked to play, to torture.

I lifted my chin and didn't move. I wouldn't take the damn glass from them.

Fabula waved Heath off and he back away, taking the glass with him. My stomach tightened. When would I be given the opportunity to have water again? No, that didn't matter.

"All right, my darling," Fabula started. "We all know how this will play out. I'll ask you to help me, you'll refuse, so I'll torture you, you'll keep refusing, and then when you're at the brink of death, you'll relent and do everything I ask of you. So why don't we save ourselves some precious time and agony?" She took a step closer. "Tell me what you know about the stone."

I stared at her, but didn't speak. I barely blinked.

Cyrene's lips curled up. "Just the answer I was hoping for. We'll have so much fun." She reached for the cell's door, and I scooted back on instinct.

Fabula lifted a hand and Cyrene stopped. "Here's the deal, my darling. You know what will happen. Do what I ask of you, or you'll regret it. I'll give you one hour to think about it."

She marched away. Cyrene glared at me, visibly disappointed at having her game ruined. Heath walked behind them, not even sparing a single glance at me, another sign that everything in this place was a big, fat lie.

Once they disappeared down the corridor, I exhaled loudly.

"Lav?" Evelyn called.

I crawled to the bars. "Yes?"

"You can't give in to her threats," she said.

Asher nodded. "Right. Whatever Fabula asks, whatever she does, don't give in to her."

Shane scoffed, his eyes closed. "Even if you give it to her, she'll find a way to torture you."

I stared at him for a moment. He was speaking from experience.

Killian halted in front of me. "You know how important that box is. She can't know how it works. Don't tell her anything."

I frowned. He was right, of course. Even if Fabula broke all of my fingers, my back, cut my flesh from my muscles, and burned my feet, I couldn't tell her.

Though, I worried I would break under the pressure. Was I strong enough?

Time passed. I couldn't tell how much, but when Fabula, Cyrene, and Heath came back, I could only guess it had been an hour.

This time, I stood in the middle of my cell, my muscles tense, my stomach in knots. Across the corridor, Killian shifted his weight from side to side. His hands clenched and unclenched, and his eyes were wide with rage.

Fabula offered me a fake grin. "So my darling, will you help me?"

"Never," I spat the word.

Her brows turned down. "So be it."

Heath produced a key from his pocket, and Deron and Tade came forward, joining him.

I braced myself.

Heath's eyes met mine. Then, he turned and unlocked Killian's cell.

They all turned their backs to me.

I advanced and grabbed the bars in my hands. "What are you doing?"

Swords in hand, Deron and Tade entered Killian's cell. Killian snarled and jumped at them. Heath pulled out a bronze key from his pocket and turned it. Killian cried out and fell to his knees.

"No!" I yelled. Heath turned the key more. Killian's arms jerked with the shock, and he fell to the side, a loud thud on the rough ground. "Let him be. It's me you want."

Deron and Tade grabbed Killian's arms, pulling him out of his cell.

I shook the bars in my grasp. "Stop it! You can't do this!"

Fabula faced me, a wicked grin on her lips now. "I told you that you would regret it."

She walked down the corridor, following the others as they took Killian away.

"No!" I screamed.

Evelyn tried talking to me, but I didn't listen. I shook the bars, I kicked them, I stepped back and tried blasting them with my magic. But nothing worked. So I shouted.

"Take me instead! It's me you want! Come back here, damn it! You filthy pieces of shit!"

The first scream reverberated through the walls, and I froze.

The second scream was a shrill thing that raised the hairs on my arms.

The third one was choked and gurgled.

Then there were no more screams.

I fell to my knees and cried.

20

I DIDN'T KNOW HOW LONG HAD PASSED, BUT WHEN THEY dragged Killian back, holding him like deadweight by his arms, it seemed like an eternity. I knelt by my cell's bars and watched with my heart in my throat. Killian's face was bloodied, his lips cracked, and his eyes swollen. Cuts marred his skin, and darkening bruises blacked his flesh.

Deron and Tade threw Killian on the floor of his cell, and Heath locked the door.

"Killian," I called, my voice breaking. He didn't move. I glanced around, ready to beg Fabula, but she wasn't there. Only Cyrene, who stood to the side, just watching. "Cyrene ..." She looked at me, disinterest clear in her face. "Please, he's really hurt." And with those damn cuts, it would take him forever to heal. "He needs blood. Please, he needs to drink from ... a rabbit, a deer, I don't know. Something."

She tilted her head at me. "What are you willing to do if we allow him to feed?"

I swallowed. "Anything. I'll do anything." Evelyn and

Asher protested, but I tuned them out. "I'll help Fabula. I'll do anything," I repeated.

"Deal." She unlocked my cell and grabbed my wrist.

"What are you doing?" I jerked against her hold.

"Don't you want to feed him?" she asked.

I stared at her. What the hell was she saying? On the other side of the corridor, Heath unlocked Killian's cell. Cyrene tugged me forward and pushed me into Killian's cell. Heath locked the door again.

"I think you know how you can feed him." Cyrene offered me a sly grin.

All of them walked away.

I stood there, frozen in place.

I had to feed Killian. Like ... from me. He had to drink my blood. For half a second, my insides turned in disgust and fear.

Then, I shoved it down and knelt beside what looked like a dead body.

"Killian," I called softly. I rested my hand on his shoulder and turned him to me. He flopped on my legs like a sack of potatoes. "Please, Killian. Get up. You need to feed."

With shaking arms, I pulled the sleeve of my sweater up but the cuffs covered the best veins. Slowly, I lay beside him. "Killian, you have to feed." I swiped my hair back and leaned closer to him. "Feed from me." I wound a hand around his head and lifted it to me. "Please, feed."

I pressed his head to my neck.

A soft groan came from him, and I almost gasped in relief. He was still alive. His lips parted, brushing against my skin, and I tensed. Any other day, his lips on my skin would have filled me with lust, but now I was desperate. He had to drink!

"Please, feed," I whispered again.

I felt the graze of his fangs and then he closed his mouth around my neck. This time, I gasped from surprise and pain. But as Killian woke up and drank from me, the pain lessened considerably, and something else replaced it, something different, something better ...

Without stopping, Killian moved. He wound his arm around my waist and laid me back, pressing his body on mine. The delicious high of the bite and the weight of his body were enough to rip a moan from my chest. I clutched Killian's shoulders and wound my legs around his waist. Holy shit, I needed him. I wanted him, and—

He retracted his teeth, and I was about to complain, but instead his warm tongue licked my skin before he placed a kiss just below my jaw.

A second later, he was standing on the other side of the cell, his wide eyes wild, and his lips red with my blood.

"What the f—?" He wiped at his lips. "What did you do?"

Pulling myself out from the wonderful haze, I sat up and stared at him. "I just saved your life."

At least it had worked. The open bruises and scratches were closed, his eyes weren't swollen anymore, and even though he wasn't in the greatest shape, he would certainly live.

"You're welcome."

Killian ran a hand through his hair and paced. "Do you know how hard it is to stop drinking human blood? Especially *your* blood? I could have killed you!" I frowned. Especially my blood? What the hell did that mean? His eyes rounded even more. "Wait ... how are you in here?"

I gulped. "I asked Cyrene."

"That wasn't free." He halted. "You told her you'll help

her." I didn't answer. "Lavinia, the hell ..." He inhaled deeply. "You shouldn't have. You should—" He stopped, slapping the stone wall with the palm of his hand.

"You're not completely healed yet," I said, containing my rage. I was mad at him for being mad at me. "If you're done grilling me for saving your goddamn life, then sit down and rest."

He glared at me. "Lavinia, we ca—"

"Stop, Killian," I snapped. "Arguing with me won't change anything now. Besides, I wouldn't change anything. If it happened again, I would make the same choice." I held his gaze, impassive.

Slowly, Killian moved. With a permanent frown, he sat down two feet from me, his back against the wall.

I was tired of fighting, of pushing and pulling, of bickering.

Feeling lost and lonely, I scooted to the corner and leaned against the wall. I closed my eyes and willed sleep to find me. My mind was reeling, but my body was hurt and tired, and I could really use a break.

I shivered as the coldness from the ground and wall sipped into my bones. It would be impossible to sleep like this.

Then, I heard a soft shuffle and felt something pressing to my side—something slightly less cold than the wall, but softer in places, and harder in others.

I spied through my eyelashes as Killian wound his arm around my waist and tugged me closer to him.

"I thought you were mad at me," I said, my voice low.

"I can be mad at you and still want to take care of you." He pulled me even closer, burying my shoulder into his chest and placing my folded legs half-over his. He hugged me tight. "You drive me crazy, you know that?"

I scoffed. "Likewise." I leaned my head on his shoulder and placed a hand over his heart. It didn't beat, but I swore I could feel it, as if it was telling me, "Hey, I'm here. Don't give up just yet."

After some time, Killian whispered, "Thank you."

"Anything for you," I said, repeating words he had said to me weeks ago. It was true and I hoped he really knew this.

He placed a kiss on the top of my head. "Rest. I'll take care of you now."

I nestled against him, enjoying this moment of reprieve. I could get used to this.

Despite all the worry, all the hurt, all the uncertainty, I relaxed in Killian's arms and slept.

21

WHEN I WOKE UP AGAIN, KILLIAN AND I WERE ON THE FLOOR, though our positions hadn't changed much—his arms were still around me, my head on his shoulder, and my legs over his.

I lifted my head and looked at him—at the hard line of his jaw and chin, at his high cheekbones, his straight nose, his long lashes, and thick eyebrows. And the small bruises marring his otherwise smooth skin. He was so, so handsome, it hurt to stare at him for so long.

"You'll bore a hole in me," Killian whispered.

I punched his side and he groaned. "Oh shit, I'm sorry." I gently pressed my hand where I had punched him. For a moment there, I had forgotten he was still hurt.

"It's okay." He looked at me. "I'm fine, really."

I frowned as something occurred to me. "Where's your box?"

"Safely hidden near the inn," he said in a low voice.

Being far from it couldn't be helping with his pain and healing.

I sat up. To me, he still looked a little pale, but that could be because he was a freaking vampire, and probably because of the dim, eerie lighting in here. Everything looked creepy and downright grave down here.

Killian sat up in front of me.

There were still more bruises on his face, neck, and arms. "How are you feeling?" I lifted the sleeve of my shirt, uncovering the cuff. Well, he could bite beside it, couldn't he? "Do you need more? Drink as much as you need."

Killian held my hand and turned it, so my palm was facing him. Holding my gaze, he lowered himself to my wrist. I inhaled deeply and braced myself for the bite. Instead, I felt his soft lips as he pressed a kiss on my skin. He lowered my arm, but didn't let go of my hand. "I'm fine now."

"Are you sure? I still see plenty of bruises, and—"

"Lavinia, I'm fine."

I stared at him. "But if you need more—"

He nodded. "I know."

His eyes didn't leave mine, and I wished I could decipher what was behind them, what I saw in there.

Then he changed. His eyes darkened, his body tensed, and he shoved me behind him. Three seconds later, I heard the footsteps approaching.

Cyrene halted before Killian's cell. Heath, Deron, Tade, and three Dark Order members stood behind her.

"It's time," she said.

Killian snarled.

I clasped his shoulders. "It's okay."

Heath unlocked the door, and Killian pushed me to the back wall. "Over my dead body," he said, the rage evident in his tone.

"A deal is a deal," Cyrene said. She didn't seem one bit worried.

I slipped my hand in Killian's, tugging him to me. He glanced at me. "It's okay," I repeated. It wasn't okay, but I had agreed to this, and like I had told him before, if given the chance, I would have made the same choice again. There was no coming back now. "Please, let me go."

His grip tightened around my hand. "Never."

I brought our joined hands to my chest. "Killian, you have to let me go before they do something worse to you or to me. I'll just tell Fabula what she wants to know and then I'll be back. They won't hurt me." At least, that was what I hoped. "Okay?" His eyes searched mine. "Let me go."

I lowered our hands and slipped my hands from his. Swallowing a sudden sob, I turned my back to him and walked out of his cell. Heath closed it instantly, and just in time—Killian crashed against the bars and reached to grab Heath's throat.

"If you hurt her, I'll kill you," Killian said, his tone deadly.

Heath looked him up and down. "I don't think you're in position to make threats." Heath grabbed my upper arm and shoved me forward.

I stumbled—I thought he did it on purpose—and Killian shouted some very colorful threats.

They took me up the stairs and back into the lodge. From the windows, I could see the faint light of the rising sun. It was morning again. I had been in those cells for over a day. Had it been only that? From how dirty and tired I felt, and how hungry, I would have guessed a week or more.

I thought I would be taken directly to Fabula, to her throne room, but I was surprised when they turned into the residential side.

"What's going on?" I asked. I was determined to hide my fear and be brave through this entire ordeal, but I couldn't help my tongue sometimes. "Where are you taking me?"

They didn't say anything until we stopped in front of my old bedroom's door. Cyrene opened the door. "Go, take a shower, eat, rest. We'll come back later this afternoon." Heath pushed me inside the room.

Before I could protest or say anything, the door was closed in my face. The lock clicked into place.

I whirled around, taking in the bedroom. It was familiar, but it felt like I hadn't been in here for at least a decade. I stared at the bathroom's door, the full closet, the bed ... and I didn't see my bag with my dagger and phone here. Not that I could do anything with those things, but they were mine, and now they were gone.

Next, my eyes landed on the tray of food resting on a side table. Now that I had seen it, my nose registered and I inhaled the smell of bacon, eggs, and cheese. My mouth watered. Like a moth lost to the light, I walked to the tray ...

And stopped. I had been asked to shower, to eat, to sleep, and yet my friends were locked in the dungeon without any of that. If we had been there for over twenty-four hours, then I could assume we hadn't eaten for at least thirty, or more, since I hadn't even eaten during the party.

I couldn't raid the kitchen and take food to them, but I could try to help them in other ways. So, despite the guilt lacing my chest, I forced myself to move. I showered in deliciously hot water; I changed into clean pants and a sweater (no dresses for me now, no matter how much the witches liked them); and I ate all the eggs, the bacon, the toast, and the cheese cubes, and drank the milk and the juice. After, my belly felt bloated, and for a moment, I thought I would throw up. Next, all I had to do was rest.

I lay in the soft bed and forced my eyes closed, but I couldn't sleep. Instead, I combed my mind for anything—a clue, a hidden passageway I might have missed, Fabula's weakness ... but nothing jumped at me. The witches had been careful with what they shared, telling me all the sweet lies I wanted to hear and nothing vital. I didn't know much about them and couldn't use anything to my advantage.

Saddened at being tricked so easily, I rolled on my side, tucked my hands under my head, and let one or two tears escape.

I was going to fight. Somehow, I would fight and win.

But first, I needed to cleanse my soul from the inside out.

SEVERAL HOURS LATER, Cyrene and the Dark Order members took me to the room behind the metal door where I had seen the box. Fabula waited for us there, seated at the head of the table, a wineglass in front of her.

And the box was in the same place I had last seen it—at the center of the table.

"I think we've been reasonable, my darling," Fabula started once I stopped in front of her. Cyrene took several steps back, as did the Dark Order. "As part of our deal, I've let you feed your beloved vampire and he's now well. Now it's your turn."

"I have one more request," I said, my voice firm, though I was trembling on the inside. I doubted they would even hear me, but if I didn't try ...

"Another request?" Fabula scoffed. She sipped from her wine. "You think you have that kind of power here?"

"Perhaps." I was gambling here. "But my request is small, considering. It shouldn't be too hard to comply with it."

She regarded me with her dark eyes. "Very well. Tell me."

"I would like for my friends to be fed," I said. "Food and water. Nothing fancy, not a lot. I know you don't want to risk having them too strong. I'm just asking for enough so they don't pass out and succumb to their weaknesses." I wanted to ask for more blood for Killian too, but I doubted they would agree to that.

Cyrene started protesting, but Fabula raised her hand. Cyrene shut up and lowered her head.

"And if I refuse?"

"Then you can take me back to my cell because I won't help you."

Fabula slapped the table. The wineglass rattled but didn't fall. Slowly, she stood and glared at me. "I'll allow it because a slice of bread and a sip of water aren't much indeed, but you're playing with fire here, my darling. Poke at me a little more and you'll get burned. Understood?"

I nodded. Fabula looked at Cyrene, who bowed her head and left the room.

I sighed in relief. A little bread and water could go a long way when you didn't have anything.

Fabula walked closer and looked down at the box. "Now, tell me, what does this stone do?"

"To be honest, I don't know much," I started, willing my voice to remain flat. "I encountered one before and was able to absorb its magic for a few moments."

Fabula's eyes widened. "You did? How?"

"I just ..." Damn it. I hadn't crafted a solid lie to tell

Fabula. My plan here was to mess with her, tell her nonsense that seemed complicated enough but true. Meanwhile, I would be trying to come up with a plan to escape from here with my friends. "I just focused on it."

"Show me."

I extended my arms at her. "These cuffs won't let me." The truth was, I thought I could do it even with the cuffs. It would have been like with the demon hunters and their magic-numbing talisman. But I didn't want Fabula to know about that.

Besides, if I got her to take the cuffs off, then I could try to use the box's magic to free my friends and escape.

She titled her head. "Do you think I'm stupid, my darling? The cuffs aren't going anywhere."

I shrugged. "Then I can't show you."

"Tell me, then!"

"I told you. I focused on the stone and its magic and willed it to me."

Fabula glared at me before closing her eyes, focusing.

Unless she also had an unexplained connection to the box, she wouldn't be able to do it. But that was one thing I wasn't willing to tell her.

Minutes passed. Fabula stayed still for a long time, focusing. After a while, she groaned and walked around the table, clearly bothered. Then she tried again.

After her fifth try, she snapped. "You're lying to me."

I shook my head. "By my mother's love, I'm not."

Fabula grabbed the wineglass, drank all of its contents, then threw it at the wall. It exploded a few feet behind me, startling me. But I stayed as still as I could.

Fabula grabbed the box in her hands. Once more, I wondered why it didn't open. What was my connection to it?

Well, perhaps this one was different and didn't open at all? No, I doubted that.

Fabula pulled her hand back, as if she would throw it at the wall too.

Cyrene, who had come back a while ago, took a step forward. "My princess, don't."

Fabula stopped. If this was really like Killian's box, then it would chip the wall, but the box would remain intact. That was another thing they didn't need to know.

With a groan, Fabula dropped the box back on the table.

"I'm tired of you," Fabula hissed at me. "We'll continue this later." She waved her hand at me. "Take her back to her bedroom."

Instantly, Heath and another Dark Order member grabbed my upper arms. They dragged me away.

Even though nothing had really happened, no progress on either side, I left the room with a small smile. Perhaps if I couldn't accomplish anything else, then at least I could make Fabula pissed.

22

———

Though it was late, I could do anything but sleep.

In desperate need of an escape plan, I turned on the bedside lamps and perused the room for anything I could use. Unfortunately, there wasn't much. The potions I had hidden in the closet were gone. There was nothing useful in the drawers, no forgotten daggers or other weapons. I searched the walls and windows—no cracks or secret doors, and the window led to the steep side of the mountain. Unless I wanted to fall to my death, I couldn't get out through there.

I could break a mirror and use a shard as a weapon, but what good would that do to me against dozens of witches and the Dark Order?

No, I needed something more.

I sat at the edge of my bed and thought of the box. I could use it, like I had used it against the demon hunters. I could absorb its magic and defeat the witches. Perhaps I was over-reaching here. Could I defeat them all with the box's power? Even if it was possible, it was risky—for my sanity. I remembered the way it had felt to have that crazy amount of dark magic inside my veins, how easy it was to bend everything to my will, to drown in that darkness, to want more and more and more ...

I shot to my feet. No, I couldn't do that again. It was hard to resist the first box's call now; imagine if I did that with a second box.

I would be lost.

A soft click came from the door. It was the middle of the night. What could Fabula want now? Unless it wasn't Fabula. It was one of the other witches who suddenly became tired of me and wanted to see me dead.

My first instinct was to grab my dagger from my boot. Shit. I had no idea where my dagger was. Instead, I backed away from the door and grabbed the long, silver candle holder from the dresser.

The door opened and two witches entered the room and closed the door behind them—Hester and Peony.

I frowned and lifted the candle holder. "What are you doing here?"

Hester placed her finger over her lips. "Shh, keep your voice down."

"And lower that thing before you hurt yourself," Peony said.

I glanced from Hester to Peony and back. Well, she had a point. It wasn't like I could hurt them with it. I put the candle holder back on the dresser. "What do you want?"

The two witches exchanged a glance.

"We would like your help," Hester said.

I blinked. "Say what?"

"It's simple," Peony said. "We want Fabula out, and you want to escape this place. Let's join forces. You help us defeat Fabula, and then we'll let you go."

I shook my head. What the hell was this? "Wait. Back up. You want to defeat Fabula?" I had heard them before, but they didn't know that. I confess, I'd thought that had been all bark and no bite. "Why?" They didn't speak right away. I crossed my arms. "Tell me or I won't even consider it."

Hester sighed. "Because Fabula has grown weak. Soft. She's an embarrassment to Nightmist."

I frowned. Wow, they thought Fabula was soft? I didn't want to think what they considered strong. "Oh-kay."

"We want her gone so we can reclaim our glory days," Peony added. "We have a few allies in the coven who will side with us."

"I hear you, but why would you need my help?" I lifted my arms and the cuffs glinted in the dim light. "I can't do shit."

"We can solve that," Hester said. "In the event of a fight—
"

"Oh, there will be a fight," Peony interrupted.

Hester continued, "We can take the cuffs off if you and your friends side with us. Your unique talents will be the tipping point."

I narrowed my eyes, thinking. "My friends include the wolf shifter, Shane."

Peony nodded. "Okay, including the wolf shifter."

I considered this. Fabula was already horrible, in my opinion. If Hester and Peony took over, what would become of the Nightmist coven? Well, that was not my problem, was it? If we were able to leave this place and never come back, then I didn't care if the new leaders were even worse than Fabula.

"So, if my friends and I help you during a battle, you'll let us go?"

"You have my word," Hester said.

"No offense, but that's not enough," I said. These were backstabbing witches, and I wanted to take all precautions I could to avoid being the next victim.

"Then we do a blood promise," Hester suggested. "If you're up for it."

I held my breath. I still had a blood promise hovering over my head, unbreakable. But this one was different. It was temporary, for a short while, until we all fulfilled our promises.

"And how do we do that?"

Hester brought her left index finger to her right palm and drew a little line across her skin. Blood bloomed from the small cut. She gestured for my hand. I extended it between us and she did the same with my palm. I hissed as she cut my skin, her nail as sharp as a knife.

She grasped my bleeding hand with hers in a tight handshake. "Now, you'll recite your promise, and I'll recite mine."

"I promise that my friends and I will fight beside you against Fabula and her allies," I said, my voice trembling. I hoped I didn't screw up this blood promise.

"And I promise I'll let you and your friends go after we defeat Fabula and her allies," Hester said, her tone firm.

A rush of magic sparked from our hands and traveled up our arms.

I gasped and pulled my hand back. I glanced at my palm as the cut closed.

Peony showed me a naughty smile. "It's done."

Hester went to the nightstand, opened a drawer, and grabbed a notepad and pen. She walked back to me and offered them to me. "Now, you should write a note."

23

AFTER HESTER AND PEONY LEFT MY BEDROOM, I TRIED sleeping, but I had a fitful night. I tossed and turned most of the time, and whenever I slept, I dreamed that Fabula was torturing Killian again. Or that she had found out about the blood promise and killed me before we could do anything.

When Fabula called me in the middle of the morning, I was tired and grumpy, but I sucked it up and went to her. I didn't want to give her reasons to take out my defiance on my friends.

This time, Cyrene took me to the throne room. A handful of witches were in there, in the TV area—Lorie, Keeva, Dot, Hester, Peony, and a couple more. But Fabula wasn't with them. She stood between the throne and a new addition to the room: a black pedestal where the box sat prettily, like an artifact in a museum.

The tiger lounged beside her, and Cyrene's raven was seated on a window frame to the side.

Fabula's eyes met mine, and for the first time since meeting her, she looked at me without any humor. "I'll get right to the point," she said as I approached her. "You will show me how to harness the magic in this stone, or I'll make all of your friends suffer. Understood?"

I dipped my chin in agreement.

Fabula made a sign to Cyrene, and she stepped forward, reaching for my hands. No, not my hands. My wrists. With that same key I had seen Heath playing before, Cyrene unlocked the cuffs. They fell on the floor with a loud clank.

I rubbed at the reddish skin around my wrists, so relieved to have those damn things off.

Cyrene leaned close. "Try anything funny, and I'll be the first to take it out on your friends."

I kept my mouth shut. I wouldn't try anything funny.

Not yet.

The four Dark Order members who always stayed behind Fabula's throne stepped forward, their hands on their swords. Another warning.

Fabula gestured to the box. "Show me. How do you harness the magic in the stone?"

"I didn't lie yesterday," I said. "The only time I did it, I just focused."

I inhaled deeply and closed my eyes. I concentrated on the box and almost instantly the pull I had felt came back, stronger now that I was beside the box. It almost brought me to my knees. In my mind, I saw myself reaching for the box, holding it, its smooth surface changing, the grooves appearing and shining, and the power flowing from it.

The magic from the box filled my veins.

I opened my eyes and brought my hands apart, creating a big ball of blue magic. I moved my hand, shaping the ball into all sorts of things—a hawk, a tornado, a knotty tree, a three-dimensional star with multiple points, Saturn, and then small stakes with sharp points. I threw my hand out and the stakes zipped across the room. They buried themselves in the wall with a flat *thunk*. And then they melted, leaving burn marks in the wall.

"Incredible," Fabula whispered.

I was amazed too. I hadn't planned this; I had no idea what I was doing. I was just feeling, just tasting the delicious and dark magic, and going with it.

Next, I pulled blue threads from the top of the box—without touching it—and created a large web between us. The web grew and grew, and finally morphed into a giant spider, twice as tall as I was.

The spider shot a web at one of the Dark Order members. It wrapped around him in an instant and took him down.

The other Dark Order soldiers pointed their swords at me. I raised my hands. "Sorry. It was a demonstration."

Fabula waved them off. "Let her continue."

From the corner of my eyes, I saw as Hester and Peony get closer and linger on the sides, like two curious spectators. The other witches were also watching us, though they stayed back.

Hester nodded once, a smooth movement I would have missed if I wasn't paying attention.

I clenched my hands, and the spider shot more webs, wrapping the tiger, Cyrene, and the other Dark Order soldiers and taking them down. The raven cawed and flew toward me. The spider shot a web at it and the bird went down.

The throne room's doors burst open. Heath, Deron, and Tade marched in, followed by a large group of witches. They stopped behind me.

"What is this?" Fabula shrieked, her eyes wild as she took in the chaos in the room.

Hester and Peony stood by my side, and Lorie, Keeva, and Dot ran to Fabula. More witches came into the room and the line was clear. The ones standing behind Fabula were loyal to her. The ones standing with Hester and Peony weren't.

Fabula stared at her son. "What the hell are you doing?"

"Forgive me, Mother," he said, though his tone had no remorse whatsoever. "I can't just stand by and watch you destroy this coven."

"What?" Fabula turned in a circle, taking in the divided groups. There were more witches on Hester's and Peony's side than I expected it, but Fabula's side was still bigger. "I'm the greatest princess this coven ever had!"

"You're delusional," Hester spat. "You've grown weak, and we're tired of it."

"Weak?" Fabula pointed at me. "Look how I tricked her! How I tortured her vampire!"

"Tricks and torture." Peony tsked. "That's child's play, Fabula, and you know it."

"I was just getting warm!" Fabula exclaimed. Her voice turned shrill, her hands shook too fast, and her eyes widened some more. She really looked delusional.

Deron shook his head. "Stop, Mother. Just surrender."

"Surrender?" She screamed and threw her hands out. Magic poured out of her, but Hester and Peony were ready for her. They created a smoky shield that absorbed most of the Fabula's magic.

Hester looked at me. "Use your spider. Immobilize as many witches as you can."

I frowned. "Where are my friends?"

Peony glanced back to the door. "They should ... ah, there they are."

In a second, Killian was by my side. Then Evelyn, Asher, and Shane entered the room. All of them sans cuffs.

"What's going on?" Killian asked in a low voice.

"I'll explain later," I told him. I nodded at Hester and Peony. "Let's do this."

The spider attacked, and its webs flew in every direction. The witches screamed and fought back. Some ran before the web could wrap around them, others attacked the spider. I felt its power dwindling with each attack. Soon, I would have to create another spider, or think of something else.

Regardless, I called more magic from the box and inhaled deeply when it filled my veins. My head spun in a dark sea for a moment, but I was able to hop on a surfboard and ride the wave.

Around me, chaos reigned. Killian zoomed from witch to witch, either incapacitating them, or killing the ones who wouldn't let go. Shane had shifted into a large, dark wolf, and attacked the witches with abandon. Evelyn threw her potions left and right, and Asher stood right beside her, brandishing his sword like a knight.

My spider took hit after hit, and it shrunk in size fast. When it was as tall as me, I let it go, and used magic bolts to fight. Each time I threw a bolt out, adrenaline rushed through me, along with the effects of the box's magic. I knew I was letting myself get lost in it, but I couldn't stop it now.

In the center of the room, Hester and Peony fought Fabula and Cyrene, who somehow had cut herself free from the spider's web. Suddenly craving suffering and death, I got closer.

In a fabulous move, Hester taunted Fabula to the right,

sidestepped, and shoved her hand into Fabula's chest. Her fingers sank into Fabula's flesh. Fabula's eyes rounded, her mouth hung open, her body went slack. Hester pulled out Fabula's heart and her body fell to the floor.

I stared, amazed and entranced by the death, the power, the darkness.

Killian appeared in front of me and grabbed my shoulders. "Lavinia." I heard him, but I was flying so high, like a freed falcon, into a cloud of darkness, diving and soaring, higher and higher. He shook my shoulders. "Lavinia, wake up!"

I stared at the beautiful vampire in front of me, I reached for him, I traced my fingertips along his cheek. He was full of darkness, like me. I could drown in him. We could drown together.

"Lavinia, please, snap out of it!" He shook my shoulders again. "Come back to me!"

I blinked.

I lowered my hands and exhaled, letting go of the box's magic. The power, the darkness, rushed out of me, and my knees weakened. Killian wrapped an arm around me and pulled me to him. He cradled my head with his other hand.

"I've got you," he whispered in my ear. "I'm here. I got you."

I fisted his shirt as a deep and empty feeling clawed its way through my chest. I pressed my cheek to Killian's chest and looked out—to the box, still intact on the pedestal, oblivious to the dying chaos around it. The box was a beacon, calling to me like a long-lost lover. My hands shook, and I itched to go to it, to hold it to me, to take more of its power. I closed my eyes and buried my face in Killian's chest.

He kissed the top of my head. "It'll be all right."

He didn't know that. Even though he was connected to his box, it wasn't like this. The box called to me. It wanted me to take it, to control it.

Now, I didn't have to resist the allure of one box, but two!

Finally, the shouts and the zaps of magic became less and less frequent. When I thought I had a good handle on myself —for now—I inhaled deeply and pulled away from Killian. But he kept his hand on my waist, like a lifeline. I needed that.

Fabula's body was on the floor, along with Cyrene's. Hester and Peony stood beside them, and Fabula's heart dripped blood from Hester's hand. I glanced around and saw several bodies littering the throne room, and several more witches on their knees, their hands tied behind their backs, and their heads low. The ones who surrendered. Evelyn and Asher stood a few feet to my left, both of them looking grim at the outcome. To my right, Shane was back in his human form, wearing a pair of pants he had stolen from the Dark Order.

"We've done it!" Peony shouted. Hester screamed, and their allies cheered.

Heath walked forward and covered his mother's body with a white sheet. Tade did the same with his mother.

My stomach sank. They had fought against their mothers. They didn't care they had been killed. No, they had sided with the murderers. I knew Hester and Peony and the ones who sided with them would be evil, but this was too much.

We had to get out of here.

I took a step closer to Hester and Peony. "I think we're done here," I told them. "I fulfilled my part of the blood promise. Now it's your turn."

Hester showed me a half-smile. "Of course. You and your friends are welcome to go." She gestured to the door.

I glanced at Killian, at my friends. Together, we walked to the door. I held my breath as we crossed the threshold. I half-expected someone to stop us. But nothing happened. We walked faster when out in the corridor, and even faster when we reached the lobby.

We walked out into the snow-covered balcony and I let out a long, relieved breath. We had made it, we had—

A force wrapped around me and I froze. "What the—?" I looked at my friends. They all seemed to be struggling against an invisible force too.

Hester and Peony walked out onto the balcony with us. Heath, Deron, Tade, and dozens of witches followed them. They spread out around the balcony, surrounding us.

"Did you really think we would let you go just like that?" Hester asked. She halted right in front of me.

"But ... the blood promise," I said, my voice strained against such powerful magic.

"Ah, yes." A wicked smile spread over Hester's lips. "*I* promised you to let you and your friends go. And look—" She spread her hands out, gesturing to the outside. "—I did."

"But I didn't promise anything." Peony toed the snow until a dark line peeked from underneath it. "It's a holding circle. You can't do anything in it."

"What? No!" I screamed in outrage. "You promised!"

Peony shook her head. "Like I said, I didn't."

I screamed as Heath came forward and slapped the cuffs back onto my wrists. The remaining Dark Order members did the same with Killian, Evelyn, Asher, and Shane.

Hester winked at me. "Now take them back to the dungeons."

—————

IT WAS LIKE DÉJÀ-VU. We tried fighting, but with the cuffs on, and with Heath abusing those damn keys that activated the painful magic in the cuff, it was hard to do anything.

I even closed my eyes for a moment and tried focusing on the box in the throne room. I wanted to reach for it, to reach for its magic, to embrace it, to have it come to me, to—

But with the cuffs around my wrists, being shoved down the stairs and almost falling face-first, and with the panic of being locked up again rising within me, it was hard to focus.

Killian tried fighting harder than all of us, and Heath was enjoying hurting him with the key and the cuffs.

"Stop, Killian," I whispered when we reached the dungeon's dark corridor. My voice was low, but with his hearing, I knew he could hear me. "We can't fight them."

He growled, shoved against a Dark Order soldier once more, but then stopped. A moment later, he was pushed back into his old cell and locked away.

As Deron opened my cell and forced me in, Peony said, "No, not her."

Oh, damn, here we go again.

Deron held my upper arm, just outside my cell, and Hester and Peony walked closer.

"We have a special treat for her," Hester said, her eyes twinkling.

"We heard from Fabula about your claustrophobia," Peony said. My chest constricted. "That would be fun to watch." She pointed to the end of the corridor. "In there."

Deron pushed me forward.

"No!" I screamed and dug my heels in the ground. Tade

came to my other side, and he and Deron lifted me from the floor, their grip tight. "Please, no!"

In his cell, Killian rammed the bars. "Let her go!"

At the end of the corridor, a small metal door sat alone against the rough wall—no windows or bars on it. A witch opened the door, and Tade and Deron pushed me toward it. I screamed and kicked my legs out, bracing them on the sides of the door.

"Such a bitch," Tade said before he punched my stomach.

The air fled from my lugs, my legs dropped like rocks, and my vision darkened. I was pushed into the tiny, dark room.

And the door closed with a definite click.

Darkness and coldness surrounded me.

I screamed.

24

My throat became raw as I screamed, as the walls closed around me, the darkness brushed its long, cold fingers down my spine and closed its claws around my neck. Without air, the scream died out, but the panic flared up. I punched the walls, clawed at them, through the solid earth. I kicked at the low ceiling, I searched for cracks or hinges on the doors —nothing.

I was in that tiny, dark closet all over again.

The echoes of past screams and fighting and begging filled my ears. I fell to the ground, my hands clamped over my ears. I couldn't do this; I couldn't do this.

I couldn't do this.

This agony, this fear, this despair.

Hours or days or years later, the door opened with a groan and light streamed in. I placed a hand over my eyes, trying to get used to it. Hands clamped around my arms and pulled me out of the cell. I blinked and focused on my surroundings. I was outside the dark cell with Tade and Deron holding me, Heath a couple of feet in front of me.

He played with the bronze keys in his hands. "Behave or I'll use this." He looked over my head and nodded.

Tade and Deron started walking, taking me with them. I forced my feet to move, but I kept tripping.

As I was taken through the corridor, Evelyn called for me, Asher asked if I was all right, Shane looked at me as if I had personally hurt him.

"Lavinia!" Killian shouted, his green eyes following me. "Lavinia," he said, softer. He reached through the bars, trying to touch me.

I moved toward him, but Tade's and Deron's grip tightened and they steered me away from him.

I felt numb as I was once more brought to my old bedroom. But this time, I wasn't left alone. Two witches stayed with me. They forced me to take a shower, to change into a dress. They fixed my hair into an intricate braid. Later, the two witches and two Dark Order soldiers escorted me to the main hall.

Dressed in a clean suit, Heath waited by the entrance. Once I stopped in front of him, he offered me his arm.

I frowned at him. "Is this a joke?"

"It is no joke," he said. He reached for my arm and looped it around his. I wanted to jerk away, but I was afraid of the consequences. He took us inside the main hall and toward the long table in the center, where two places had been set for dinner. "Even though spending time with you was part of my mother's plan, I do like you. I could see myself falling for you, if not for your deceit."

Heath let go of my arm and pulled out a chair for me. Again, I shook on the inside from the moments of agony I had spent inside that tiny cell, and of anger for this man who was still toying with me.

I thought of Killian, Evelyn, Asher, and Shane. I couldn't take a misstep now or they would suffer.

I sat down. Heath pushed my chair toward the table, then sat beside me.

A human servant came from the corridor leading to the kitchen with a wine bottle and a small tray of hors d'oeuvres. She set them on the table and retreated to the corner, waiting for us to call her again.

I watched her for a moment. She couldn't be older than me, and yet she seemed so meek, so weak. So hopeless. I remembered the other human servants Fabula had killed during that ceremony and my stomach curdled.

I need to get away from here.

But I couldn't do it without Killian and my friends.

Heath poured wine into our glasses. He took a healthy sip, then waited, watching me. Suppressing a groan, I picked up my glass and forced myself to take a sip—a small one.

"My dear Lavinia," Heath started. He took my hand in his.

My brows slammed down. "What the hell are you doing?"

He brought my hand to his lips, but before he could kiss it, I pulled away.

A growl came from the other side of the room. I gasped as Killian was brought into the room, six witches around him, their hands at the ready for a spell should he try anything. One of the witches picked up a chair from a table and turned it so it had a full view of Heath and me. The witches jerked Killian into the seat. When he fell into the chair, they tied ropes around his ankles and his shoulders.

He stared at Heath with a murderous glint. "I'll kill you."

Heath waved him off. "I heard that before." He reached for my hand again.

"Don't even think about it," I said with a hiss.

"But I brought him here for the show!" He leaned closer, making me lean back to get away from him. "It'll be fun to make him jealous."

I gaped at him. "You're insane."

Heath shrugged, but straightened. "The truth is, I wanted him here so you'll behave."

Hester and Peony came into the room. I stared at Hester's hands—she held the box as if it was a gold bar. I frowned. She was touching the damn box and nothing was happening. I had no idea if this one would open if I touched it, but I thought it would. Otherwise, why would it call to me with the allure of a siren?

Hester placed the box in front of me. "Tell us about the stone," she said as she and Peony took the seats across from me.

"I showed Fabula how to do it," I said. "You were there; you saw it."

"We tried replicating it and none of us could harness the magic," Peony said. "Most of us can't even feel it."

"There's a missing piece," Heath said. "Something to activate it. And you're hiding it from us."

Hester clasped her hands over the table. "You will tell us what it is."

I lifted my chin. "What if I don't?"

Heath nodded his chin. Deron and Tade walked to Killian. Deron unsheathed his sword and leveled it over against Killian's sternum.

"Wait, no!" I cried.

But Deron didn't stop. He dragged the sword's tip across Killian's heart, drawing blood.

Killian hissed. I gasped.

"It's okay, Lavinia," Killian said through gritted teeth. "Don't do what they are asking. Don't give them anything."

Heath signaled again. This time, Deron pushed the tip of his sword in the center of Killian's chest. He groaned in pain, trying to hide it from me.

I shot to my feet. "Stop! Stop!" I glanced at Heath. "I'll do it. I'll show you."

Heath lifted his hand. Deron retreated from Killian.

Killian's ragged breathing hurt my heart. "Lavinia, no."

"It's okay," I whispered, more to myself than to him. I wanted to bargain with Heath, Hester, and Peony. If I showed them what to do, they would let Killian alone, but I had tried that before and they had tricked me.

Now, it was my turn to trick them.

"There's one thing I wasn't telling you," I started. They all watched me with interest, including the witches around Killian, and the other Dark Order soldiers in the room. I met Killian's eyes. Damn, how I wished he could read my mind. But he seemed to understand what I wanted, what I was going to do. He sucked in a sharp breath and gave me a small nod of his head. I looked at the box in front of me. "This isn't a stone." I reached toward it. "It's a box."

My fingertips grazed the box's surface. Instantly, lines sank into its sides and white light shone. The box trembled and opened.

Thick smoke escaped from the open box, surrounding everyone at the table.

"What is this?"

"What is happening?"

"I can't see anything!"

While they all shouted to each other, I reached into the

smoke and touched the shoulder of the person crouched on the table, beside the open box.

A snarl echoed.

"Shh, it's okay," I said. The smoke cleared a little, and I saw dark eyes and dark hair framing a deadly face. A woman. "We've been captured. Help me fight the other witches, and then I'll give you your freedom."

I didn't wait to see what the woman was exactly, or if she would agree to my request. I had to believe she would, or my plan was lost.

Taking advantage before the smoke cleared, I barreled into Heath and broke a dinner plate on his head. Dazed, he fell into his seat, and I took the bronze keys from him. I got rid of the cuffs around my wrists while I ran toward Killian. The smoke was clearer here and the witches and Tade and Deron saw me coming. They swung their weapons at me.

With my life on the line, my magic reacted. I created a dozen blue bolts, turned them into ice stakes, and threw them at our enemies.

The witches, Tade, and Deron ducked, but they weren't fast enough. The stakes impaled Tade's arm, Deron's shoulder, and ... the witches didn't make it. I pushed past them and unlocked the cuffs around Killian's wrists. He shot up and turned to me. He embraced me tight.

"As much as I am enjoying this, we don't have time." I stepped back from his arms and pressed the bronze keys to his hand. "You're faster than me."

He nodded and turned first to Deron and Tade—he broke their necks, then disappeared in a flash.

And I turned to a mostly smokeless room.

The woman had heeded my plea and fought against our

enemies. I took a second to look at her—she had pale skin, long limbs, and pointed ears. A fae?

She seemed as wild and crazed as Killian had been when he first got out of the box—she had torn pants and a tee, worn boots. Her messy braid was way past her butt, and scars covered her exposed arms.

She held a shadow sword in her hands and brandished it like a practiced warrior. I gasped when I saw Peony's body at her feet, along with two other witches. Heath limped away, a gash across his stomach, and Hester cowered in the corner, a shield in front of her.

More witches entered the main hall and they didn't waste time—they attacked the fae. I called my magic again, throwing a few bolts here and there, mostly to distract the witches attacking the fae, and giving her cover fire.

The fae leaped from the table, moving around the room like a ninja. I ran to the table, opened two of the cloth napkins, wrapped the box in them, and hugged it to my chest. I had to hide this box in a secure location so I could join the fae, help her. It wasn't fair I had freed her and left her to deal with our enemies by herself.

At least, I was relieved she was powerful. If a weak fae had come out ... we would have been dead already.

Before I could think of a place to hide the box, a rush of wind caressed me. Killian. He joined the fae, fighting the witches that kept coming into the room.

I lifted my hand to send a bolt of magic toward Hester, who chased after the fae, when a hand wrapped around my waist, and the point of a blade pressed against my neck. I gasped and almost dropped the box.

"Where do you think you're going?" Heath asked, his ragged voice near my ear. He moved his arm to get a better grip on me, and I saw the blade—my dagger used against me.

Killian froze. He turned to us, his eyes black, his fangs showing. One second, he was on the other side of the room, and the next, he was beside me—my dagger in his hand, and Heath's throat in the other.

"I told you I would kill you," Killian snarled. He twisted Heath's neck until it cracked. I gasped again and took a step back so Heath's body wouldn't fall on me. Killian's fangs retracted and the black lines around his eyes disappeared. He stared at me. "Are you okay?"

I nodded, still breathless. All this killing, all this danger. I was done with it. I just wanted to leave!

"Where's Evelyn and Asher? And Shane?" I asked, my voice quaking.

"They went to get the dragon's teeth," Killian told me. "And Shane shifted and is killing every witch in sight." A growl came from the hallway outside the main hall. "There." He pointed and we saw a gray shape leap in front of the door and disappear on the other side.

From my left, Hester screamed, throwing her hands out at us.

"Watch out!" I grabbed Killian's arm, tugging him out of the way.

Hester cast another spell.

Without thinking, I took my dagger from Killian, spun out of the way, and buried it in Hester's gut.

Her eyes widened, her mouth opened and closed, her body became heavy. "You had so much potential," she whispered before collapsing.

I pulled my dagger from her stomach and stepped back, disgusted and even more tired of all of this.

"We need to go," I told Killian. "The witches won't stop coming. We need to find the others and retreat."

He nodded.

Holding the box in my arms, I ran to the fae. When she saw me coming, she raised a wall of shadows and turned to me, her black eyes blazing. "What in the shadows is going on?"

"I'll explain later," I told her. "Right now, I need you to do something, like … can you create a diversion? We need to keep these witches busy and run."

She frowned. "I can trick them for a few seconds with something like this." She pointed to the wall behind her. "It won't hold for long, though."

"All we need is a few seconds. I'll shout for you when it's time."

"Twyla," she said. "That's my name."

"I'm Lavinia." I nodded at her once more and joined Killian on the other side of the room, where he fought half a dozen witches.

Shane leaped in his wolf form, ripping through the throng of witches effortlessly—it would've been a beautiful sight, if it weren't for all the blood and killing.

Evelyn and Asher found us, our bags around their shoulders, and the box with the dragon teeth in Evelyn's arms. "What's the plan?"

"We create a diversion and run," I told them.

She plucked vials from her pockets. "I've stopped by the potions room." She handed me a couple. "Throw them far from us when you're ready."

I glanced at my friends. "Let's do this." I threw the vials along the entrance of the main hall. Thick red smoke filled the air. "Twyla, now!"

The shadow sword in Twyla's hand disappeared. Groaning, she brought her hands up. A huge wave of shadow washed over the witches, pushing them back.

She ran to us.

We raced past the back door, leading to a smaller hallway that connected to the kitchen and the service rooms. Witches followed, but Evelyn threw the potions at them. The red smoke spread, and the witches screamed when they reached it.

"It's a magical acid," she explained.

Clever.

We didn't slow down as we passed the stunned human servants. But I almost did. I almost stopped and asked them to leave, to run, to escape and be free. These people weren't themselves, though. I noticed that during the full moon ceremony when the humans stood there and let Fabula kill them. They had been enchanted, and unfortunately, I didn't have the time or the power to save them all.

We went down the stairs to the underground garage. Killian grabbed a car key from the hooks beside the door and clicked it. The lights of the Hummer blinked. We hopped in it—Killian behind the wheel, me in the passenger side. Evelyn, Asher, and Twyla took the backseat, and Shane hopped into the trunk.

The path was covered in ice and snow, but the Hummer had good traction and Killian sped away from the lodge.

In the back, Shane shifted back to his human form. "We made it," he said, his voice low. "I got out."

I glanced back at him. "You said you had been here for several months. Do you know how many?"

"About six months, I think," he said, his eyes grave. He ran a hand through his shaggy hair. "Hm, you know, I'm naked here. Not that I mind. Wolves are used to that, but I thought you would. Anyone have any pants to spare?"

"You're lucky I stopped to get our things." Asher dug through the duffel bag at his feet and threw black pants and a white T-shirt to Shane.

"Thanks," the wolf shifter said.

I was straightening in my seat when Twyla spoke up. "Just hang on a minute. Now that the fighting is over, can someone explain to me what in the shadows is going on?"

25

———

After a quick pit stop at the inn to get the rest of our things and Killian's box, which he had hidden in the woods behind the inn, we drove nonstop for hours in the middle of the night.

We told Twyla about what we were doing at that lodge, about my connection to the boxes, that Killian had also been in a box, and that twenty years had passed since she had been put in there—at least, that was what we assumed since, from what Delia had told us, Killian had been the last supernatural placed in a box before she fled with them.

Twyla was quiet for most of the trip. I wanted to ask her how Soren's warlocks found her and what happened before she was taken to the box, but she seemed so lost, so confused, I kept quiet.

We stopped at a rest stop when the Hummer was almost out of gas. Killian compelled a poor car owner, and we switched cars—this time, we picked one with three rows so Shane had a seat.

We drove southeast, aiming to get back into the United

States, but before we crossed the border, Evelyn and Asher asked to hop out. I didn't understand why they wanted to leave, but they said they had more dragon bones to track.

When the sun was rising, we stopped at a train station at their request. They wanted to take the train back to Calgary, where they had some resources hidden.

Evelyn, Asher, Killian, and I exited the car, but Shane and Twyla waved at them from the inside.

I turned to Evelyn. "I'm sorry I lost myself there for a moment."

She shook her head. "Don't worry about it. I understand what happened and I can't really blame you. I'm just glad you snapped out of it." She pulled me into a hug. "I'm sorry they used your mother to trick you."

I let out a sigh. "Me too." I pulled back and smiled at her. "I hope you find what you're looking for."

"Thanks," Evelyn said.

"We wish good luck to you too," Asher said. He took my hand and gave it a tight handshake. "With these boxes, you'll need it." He glanced at Killian. "Take good care of her."

Killian scoffed. "As if anyone needed to tell me that." The guys grasped forearms, and I choked up.

Evelyn motioned to her cell phone. "Keep in touch."

I nodded. "I will. And if you need anything ..."

"I know," she whispered.

They waved at us and walked away. I stayed in the same spot by the car as they got in line to buy train tickets. I didn't know why, but it was like losing them. I had lost so many people already; it hurt to leave them behind.

Killian tugged at my sleeve. "We should go."

I nodded and got in the car again.

Another three hours on the road, I convinced Killian to

stop for breakfast. He might not need to eat food, but we did. He stopped at a diner at the edge of a small town. He went hunting while Shane, Twyla, and I got a booth beside the diner's wide window.

When we left the witches' lodge, we had asked Shane what he wanted to do. He said he wanted to get away from there. I hadn't pushed the subject. As for Twyla, I didn't really give her a choice. Even if she wanted leave, I was connected to her box and I was taking it to DuMoir Castle. There, we would figure out what to do, and then hopefully, she and Killian would be free.

She didn't seem happy with it, though.

Shane ordered a huge cheeseburger even though it was ten in the morning, Twyla asked for a salad wrap, and I had waffles and tea. Several minutes later, we were almost done with our food, and Killian hadn't come back yet.

"So, if I stay with you, I'll be heading to a castle full of vampires?" Shane asked, surprising me.

"Vampires and witches, from what I heard," I told him.

Twyla frowned. "But ... vampires and witches are enemies." She glanced out the window, and I was sure she was thinking of Killian and me.

"Well, a lot has changed in the last twenty years," I said. I gave her a quick summary of how not all supernaturals were evil and that different species were now allies.

"That's ... crazy," she whispered.

"Tell me about it," Shane said. "I haven't been away for that long, but where I came from, wolf shifters don't mix with vampires. In fact, my pack has always hated them."

I sighed. "If you aren't comfortable with where you're going, Shane, you're welcome to leave."

He crossed his big arms and frowned. Now that he didn't

look beaten to death in that cell, I could see he was big, with thick arms and wide shoulders, wider than Killian's. He was also almost as tall as Killian. He was wearing a jacket now, which added to his bulk. Though, his beard and hair were still in need of some TLC.

"I can't go home," he grumbled. Then, he offered a shiny smile and looked at Twyla. "How about I bunk with you, sweetheart?"

Twyla wrinkled her nose. "Ew. As if fae would mix with werewolves."

"Wolf shifters," Shane said.

Twyla rolled her eyes.

I smiled. This was almost normal ... we were just missing Killian. I glanced out the window, wondering about him. If he didn't show up in a few more minutes, I would worry for real.

Half an hour passed and I was done waiting. "Let's go."

I paid for our meal and walked outside, the others following me. I stopped by the car and looked out. Where the hell could he be?

I turned to Shane. "Can you hear him in the woods?"

"My hearing in this form is better than most, but it's even more enhanced when I shift," Shane explained. "If you want, I can shift and look for him."

I bit the inside of my cheek. "I would really appreciate that."

Shane nodded and started for the woods.

Wind rushed past me and Killian showed up two feet from me. "We need to go. *Now*." He grabbed my hand and opened the car's door.

"Wait, what happened?" I jerked my hand from his. "Where were you?"

"Running from warlocks," he told us. I gasped. "They will be here in less than fifteen seconds. We need to *go*."

Twyla knew what the warlocks meant, and Shane had heard they had been after us—me—when I told them what happened to us earlier. The four of us entered the car and Killian gunned it. He drove onto the road and sped up.

In the distance, hooded figures emerged on the road, their cloaks billowing behind them, forming a human barricade across the road.

Killian stepped on it. "Brace yourselves."

Oh, shit. I pressed my hands to the dashboard. In the backseat, Shane held on to the grab handle, and Twyla grasped the seat belt across her lap.

The anticipation of the impact built up, and I felt a scream rising in my throat as we got closer.

Five meters from the line, the warlocks raised their hands in unison.

And our car flew. The tip rose toward the sky and leaped over the warlocks, giving one full flip in the air. My stomach turned with it, and I saw stars. The car smashed back on the road and everything went black for a moment.

I came to with hands holding my arms, dragging me out of the turned car. My head screamed, my vision blurred. What the hell? I blinked, trying to make sense of my surroundings.

The warlocks, the car flip.

I gasped and yanked at the hands dragging me away from the car. One of the warlocks tightened his grip and the other hissed. "Quiet, girl."

I looked over my shoulder. The car was turned upside down, the trunk destroyed, and smoke coming from the engine. I could see Killian, Twyla, and Shane inside, unconscious and covered in blood.

My breath caught. "No," I whispered. Another warlock reached inside the car and got the duffel bag that had been tucked under my seat. He opened it and smiled—the boxes were in there. "No."

A grunt came from the car.

"Set it on fire before the others wake up," a warlock said.

"No!" I cried.

A warlock stopped beside the car and lifted his hands. I had one second to think, one second to act. I closed my eyes and focused on the boxes. Even if it hurt Killian and Twyla, even if later it would make it hard for me to resist them, I had to do it.

It was our only chance.

In my mind, I reached for the boxes.

A yelp came from behind me, and I snapped my eyes open.

The warlock in charge of the fire lay in the road, at Killian's feet. The black lines adorned his dark eyes, and his fangs protruded when he snarled. My heart leaped in relief. He was alive!

But he was pissed.

He zipped to the warlock with the boxes.

Another warlock threw a dark bolt at Killian. It hit him in the shoulder, driving him back.

"Stop it!" I jerked against my captors, but they were stronger than me. They kept dragging me away, toward the woods.

Two more warlocks joined the other one and the three of them attacked Killian. In his super speed, he zigzagged their strikes, losing most of them, but not all.

Another bolt got him in the leg and Killian staggered, losing his momentum.

A warlock conjured a powerful dark bolt and aimed at Killian.

I held my breath.

The zoom of a car reached my ears three seconds before it drifted to a stop right beside Killian. Three more SUVs followed the first one.

A man with black hair and striking blue eyes climbed from the first car. He dashed forward to the warlock with the dark bolt in his hands, just as fast as Killian. He grabbed the warlock's head and snapped it.

The warlock's body kissed the road and the vampire smoothed his hands down his dark suit. "Anyone else?"

Killian stared at the vampire standing a few feet from him. "Drake," he whispered in disbelief.

Two beautiful women stepped out of the first car, a blond one in her twenties, and another one, older, in her forties or fifties. Both of them walked toward Killian.

"Killian," the older one said, her tone heavy. "It has been so long."

He paled. "Acalla."

"Hi, Killian," the blond one said, catching his attention. "I'm Thea." She lifted her head and looked at me. "We're here to help."

26

———

THE WARLOCKS HOLDING ME RAN INTO THE WOODS WHILE THE other warlocks attacked Lord Drake, Queen Thea, and Acalla.

Oh my God, I couldn't believe they were here.

I jerked, pulling my weight down to slow the warlocks, but one of them punched my cheek. My head snapped to the side; my vision blurred instantly. The pain spread through my face, and I lost control over my body.

"Where do you think you're going?"

The warlocks stopped short and faced Drake, who had appeared in front of us. They let me go and I fell on my butt. I pressed a hand to my cheek. Shit, it hurt!

Hands found me again and I jerked to the side.

"It's okay," Queen Thea said. She crouched beside me. With a small smile, she reached over and touched her fingertips to my cheek. A cooling sensation spread. The pain numbed almost completely and my vision returned to normal.

I sighed in relief. "Thank you."

"My pleasure." She took my hand in hers and helped me stand.

I glanced around. There were at least ten vampires and five witches, rounding up the warlocks. In the distance, I could see Acalla tending to Twyla and Shane, who were seated on the open trunk of one of the SUVs. They seemed banged up, but okay, though Twyla seemed to be yelling at Acalla. Of course—they had met before. Acalla had been there when Twyla was forced inside the box. Just like Killian.

To the side, Lord Drake and Killian talked in hushed tones. Killian pointed in my direction and Drake nodded. Killian's hands clenched, and his jaw tightened. Drake rested a hand on Killian's shoulder.

"They have a lot to talk about," Queen Thea said.

"I bet," I whispered.

She offered me an empathetic smile. "You all have been through so much."

I frowned. "How did you know where to find us?"

"Almae had a vision of Killian, the box, you ... and more."

"Almae?" I asked, confused. Who was that?

Queen Thea gestured to the witch who had left Twyla and Shane and was now walking toward us. "That's Almae."

"Wait ... but Killian called her Acalla." She had been the one who created the boxes with Soren, the one who could control them.

The older witch joined our small circle. "Once upon a time, I was called Acalla. When I was running from Soren, I changed my name to Almae."

Something clicked in my mind. "Oh! I went to see the Lightgrove witches several weeks ago. They told me a powerful witch called Almae was going to visit them, that maybe she could help me." I gasped. I couldn't believe Acalla and Almae were the same witch.

"My dear, there's more," Almae said. Tears brimmed in her eyes, and she pulled me into a tight hug. "I finally found you."

I stilled, my hands to my sides. "W-what?"

She pulled back a little so she could look at me. "You look so much like your mother." A tear escaped and she wiped it away. I stared at her. "My dear, your mother was my younger sister."

What?

I wanted to rub at my ears, slap my face, pinch myself. This was crazy. Too much. I had been tricked before. The Nightmist had played with me ...

But as I stared at Acalla, I saw it. She had the same eyes as my mother, the same nose. Even her hair, now graying, looked the same. I inhaled deeply. Oh, God, I had gone from not having a family, to suddenly having an aunt? And she wasn't just anyone. She was a powerful witch, one who had visions, and who had created the boxes—

I gasped. "That's why I can open the boxes. Because you made them." An even more surprising thing occurred to me. "Oh, shit, you can break the blood promise."

She nodded. "I saw that in my vision. Because we shared the same blood, I can mostly definitely break the blood promise."

I inhaled deeply and my chest shook as a quick sob took over me. I couldn't believe this was happening. "Holy shit," I whispered. Then slapped my hand over my mouth. I was in the presence of my *aunt* and a powerful witch queen.

"Oh, don't worry," Queen Thea said with a grin. "We curse all the time."

I chuckled. My feelings were raw and a complex mix of relief and joy and a little confusion.

Acalla—or Almae—retreated a step, but held one of my hands between hers. "But before I can break anything, we should get you to DuMoir Castle. It's not safe here."

"That's true," Queen Thea said. "We should go." She gestured to a witch with copper hair wearing an elegant pencil skirt and blouse. If I didn't know better, I would have assumed this witch was a successful businesswoman on Wall Street. She stood beside a tall blond man, who didn't seem to be a vampire like the others. The witch and the man walked toward us. "Elisa, I'll accompany Lavinia, Killian, and the others back to the castle. Please stay and make sure these warlocks are dealt with."

"Of course," the witch said. "Zad will help me." The blond man tipped his head in a teasing bow.

One corner of Queen Thea's lips tugged up. "I wouldn't expect anything less."

Almae pulled me toward the first SUV.

When she opened the door for me, Killian appeared by our side. He stared at her for a hot minute, then his gaze softened as he shifted toward me. "Are you okay?"

I nodded. "You?"

He lifted a shoulder. "I'll survive." Slowly, he reached for me and entwined his fingers with mine. My heart skipped a beat. "At least now we're safe. *You're* safe." He squeezed my hand.

I smiled at him.

So much had happened in a short time, I still couldn't wrap my head around half of the things. I would need a week to rest and then another week to make sense of everything.

"Lavinia," Killian started, his voice grave, more serious.

"What?" I held on to his hand in mine. "What is it?"

He stared for a slow minute. Finally, he opened his mouth to say something else—the sound of a door snapping shut startled us.

Lord Drake rounded the car and opened the driver's door. "Let's roll out!"

27

DURING THE FIRST THIRTY MINUTES IN THE SUV, WE TALKED A lot. Killian told Drake what had happened to him. Almae added details she remembered from when Soren had abducted him. And then I realized Almae had been a Silverblood witch. I asked her if my mother had been one too.

"Yes," Almae said. "She was a Silverblood witch, which means you're one too."

I stared at Thea in the passenger seat beside Drake. She was my coven's queen. Holy shit.

I frowned. "Do you know why my mother left?"

Queen Thea twisted in her seat and looked back at us. "I was a toddler when she left, but from the digging we did, we think Zaira met your father and fell in love. At that time, demon hunters were supposed to kill witches. We believe she left the coven to be with him."

That made sense. The demon hunters had mentioned my father had disappeared and then they found him with my mother. It seemed he too had chosen her over his people.

That was true love.

I felt proud and a little jealous.

The conversation dwindled, and despite myself, I leaned back in the comfortable seat of the customized SUV and slept most of the ride to DuMoir Castle.

"Lavinia, wake up." Almae gently tapped my shoulder. I woke up with a start.

I rubbed at my eyes, glancing around. It was darkening outside, the sun almost gone, which meant we had been on the road for hours—and I had crashed hard. Lord Drake still drove the SUV with Queen Thea beside him. They held hands over the center console. I sat on the right of the back-seat with Almae in the middle, and Killian to her left. Shane and Twyla were in the third row.

"I'm up," I mumbled, still sleepy. I guess the energy and adrenaline of the last few days had simply faded, and I was now running on fumes.

"Then look out the window," Almae said.

I did.

My mouth hung open as I took in the cobblestone road that ran through what looked like an 1800s village, with small buildings and houses. I frowned, noticing electric lamps illuminated the stone-paved streets but no people anywhere.

"Lower-ranked vampires lived here before," Killian said, looking out the window too.

"A lot of vampires died during the DuMoir Battle," Lord Drake said as he drove through the village. "The ones who survived came to live at the castle with us. But we keep the village running for when our numbers go back up."

We crossed over a bridge that spanned a lake, curving along the edge of the village. A long, winding road led uphill. We rounded the last curve on the road and it opened to a lush garden beyond, and behind it all, the large stone castle. I gaped at it, taking in the turrets, balconies, and windows.

"It's gorgeous," I whispered.

"What happened to the east side?" Killian asked. "The stone looks different."

"Half of the castle was destroyed during the battle," Lord Drake said. "We rebuilt it, but despite the best architects, engineers, and magic, we still notice the difference."

I, for one, had no idea what they were talking about.

Lord Drake drove through the garden and stopped the SUV in front of wide stone stairs that led up to the huge dark wooden doors—they had to be at least sixteen feet high!

Exiting the SUV, we climbed up the stairs—I had the bag with the boxes slung over my shoulder and Almae carried my bag with my things. Two vampires in dark uniforms stationed outside the doors bowed at Lord Drake and Queen Thea—then I realized: should I bow to them too?—and opened the heavy doors for us.

The foyer was as grand and luscious as the outside with tall windows, shiny floors, immense chandeliers, and a dreamy wraparound staircase.

Many male vampires lined the front of the stairs.

"The princes," Almae whispered to me.

Oh. Killian was supposed to be one of them, wasn't he? Before Soren took him, he had been sent for what he believed had been the last test.

The princes greeted Killian, and Queen Thea introduced them to me: Dorian, Aston, Gray, Cain, and Patrick.

"You're a prince," Killian said as he shook Prince Patrick's hand. Like all princes, Prince Patrick looked good in his impeccable suit. From the slight wear around his eyes, I guessed he had been in his late thirties when he was turned.

Prince Patrick shrugged. "It has been a while."

I could sense the tension rolling around them in waves. There was something there.

Lord Drake took three steps up the staircase and turned to all of us. "Killian, we're glad you're back home. We have much to talk about. Tonight, we'll let you rest, but tomorrow night, we'll celebrate—and we'll finally crown you Prince Killian."

I stared at Killian, who stood still as a statue. I wanted to go to him, to poke him, to hug him, but there were too many people between us. The other princes patted his shoulder, congratulating him.

Queen Thea stood beside Lord Drake. "And we're also glad for our new friends, Lavinia, Twyla, and Shane. Please, make yourselves at home."

"Prince Cain," Lord Drake called one of the princes. "We have one guest room prepared for Lavinia, but we need two more."

Prince Cain gave one sharp nod of his head. "I'm on it, my lord." He turned to Shane and Twyla. "Please, follow me." He went up the stairs.

Before following him, Shane and Twyla glanced at me. I offered them what I hoped was an encouraging smile.

Almae took my hand in hers and I forgot about Shane and Twyla. "Come with us," she said.

I followed her and Queen Thea to a large sitting room to the right. It opened up to another even larger sitting room, and then to a mash of a sunroom and a greenhouse. The walls and high ceilings were made of glass with thin metal structures, and there were plants, trees, and herbs everywhere. Stone paths wound around the flowers and bushes, and every so often, there was a wooden bench or a long wooden table with books and tools.

"This is a potions room," I said as they took me to the center of the large room, where it opened to a clearing with a round stone pavement.

"It's my corner in the castle," Queen Thea said. "The Silverblood witches have their own estate, but I spend a lot of time here. For obvious reasons." She showed me a brief smile. "When I'm not helping Drake with political and bureaucratic matters, I come here and play with my plants."

"Mommy!" a child shouted from somewhere. I looked toward the sound of the voice; a little girl ran into the stone clearing, her arms wide.

"My baby," Queen Thea said, lowering herself and receiving the child with open arms. The little girl launched herself at the queen, who caught her, stood up, and spun with her. The little girl giggled. She was beautiful with luscious dark curls, brilliant green eyes, and pale skin.

"This is Aurora," Almae told me. "She's Thea's and Drake's daughter." I frowned. I didn't know much about vampires and witches, but I didn't think that vampires could procreate. "And she's also the most powerful witch who ever existed."

This little girl was the most powerful witch ever? So young? That was hard to believe.

Thea put Aurora down and she smiled at me. "I know it's hard to understand," she said, sounding way older than she looked. "Sometimes, I feel uncertain too. But I know I have special supernaturals guiding me down the right path."

My jaw fell to the floor.

"Yes, she surprises us all the time," Almae said.

"That she does." Thea ran a hand over Aurora's curls. "All right, Lavinia, are you ready to break the blood promise?"

I swallowed hard. "Yes, Queen Thea." I took the duffel bag from my shoulders and placed it on the floor beside my feet. Almae dropped my other bag beside it.

"Oh, please, no need to call me queen," she said, her tone steady and calm. "Just Thea is fine. Same for Drake. Don't call him *Lord* Drake unless it's official business in front of others; otherwise, he loathes it."

I smiled. I liked these people more and more by the minute.

"Let's get started." Almae grabbed my elbow and pulled me to the center of the stone circle. "There isn't much to it. We need to do what your mother first did, but once your magic is released, we don't know how you'll react to it." She gestured to Thea. "That's why we're here, away from the others, and ready to contain anything, if needed."

I pressed my lips tight. "You're scaring me."

"There's nothing to be scared of," Almae said. "I just like being prepared. That's all."

I nodded.

Thea handed a small dagger, no longer than my index finger, to Almae. She cut her right palm. "I hereby undo the blood promise calling for keeping Lavinia's magic hidden and only reachable when absolutely necessary." She passed the dagger to me. For the second time in a couple of days, I cut my palm for another blood promise. "This was your mother's promise, not yours, so you don't have to say anything. Just accept it." She offered me her hand.

"Oh-kay." I took it.

Her blood mixed with mine and a bright light flashed

from our joined hands. I felt the magic zipping up my arm like hundreds of ants crawling over my skin.

She pulled her hand back. "It's done."

I glanced at the thin line of blood on my palm, then at her. "That was it?"

Almae's brows turned down. "It didn't work?"

I shook my head. "I don't feel—" I gasped as my gut tightened and my chest erupted in a million sparks on the inside. Colors filled my vision and I was suddenly floating on cloud nine.

The force was so strong, so intense, so heavy, my knees weakened, and I fell to the ground. My arms lit up and my hands looked like flashlights.

"She's losing control," someone said.

Hands grabbed my shoulders and another hand pressed against my chest. Strong magic jerked into me, making me gasp again. It was similar to mine, but different. My magic resisted it, fought it, but after a while, a hum filled my veins, and my power slowed down.

I blinked and the colors were gone. My arms and hands didn't shine anymore. I still felt a massive pressure inside me, as if too much lingered. I wouldn't be able to contain it for long.

Another force found me.

A sweet, sweet call.

I glanced at the duffel bag on the ground. The boxes' call was different now. Steadier, but not stronger. It was easier to feel it, to want it, to—

Aurora picked up the bag and took several steps back. "The boxes are calling to her."

I shrank into myself, ashamed that I had been on my

knees, crawling to the boxes, and I hadn't even noticed until Aurora took them out of range.

I sat down, feeling like I wasn't myself.

"Lavinia, talk to me," Almae asked. She was crouched beside me. "What are you feeling?"

I pressed a hand to my chest. "Too much magic. I can't ... I can't control it. I feel like it's going to burst."

She nodded. "That's expected. You're not used to having your full powers."

"But I'm a half-witch. My powers were never supposed to be strong."

"For some reason, you're not fifty-fifty. You're a lot more witch than demon hunter."

My brows knotted. That made sense. Demon hunters were supposed to be faster and stronger and have more stamina than humans. I sure didn't have any of that.

"We should have waited until tomorrow morning to do this," Thea said. "Now she won't sleep with her powers like that."

"It's okay," Almae said. "I'll give her a potion to numb her magic for a few hours."

That sounded like a good idea.

"There's also the boxes' call," I said, though it pained me. The boxes' magic didn't want me to share anything, to tell her anything. They wanted me to touch them, to absorb them, to harness their powers, by myself. Just me. To be powerful, strong, unstoppable ... I shook my head.

"I've used their powers before. Killian's box when the demon hunters attacked us several weeks ago, and Twyla's box a couple of days ago, when we were trapped in the Night-mist coven. Since then, I can feel them calling me." I rubbed at my chest. "But now, it's steadier, stronger, in a way."

But not louder. It was hard to understand what was going on. I glanced at the bag in Aurora's arm and forced my eyes closed.

Almae placed a hand on my shoulder. "It's okay, my dear. We'll figure out how to counteract the boxes' call. Meanwhile, we'll put them in a safe place. Don't worry." She took my hands in hers and helped me up. "And tomorrow we'll train. I'll help you master your magic."

"We'll also talk about the boxes and figure out how to deal with them," Thea said.

"And how to sever my connection to them," I added.

She nodded. "That too."

Once more, Almae took my hand in hers. "Come on. Let's make you some nice potions and put you in bed."

Even though I felt like a bomb ready to explode, I was also exhausted and dirty. Putting this day behind me sounded like a great idea.

28

ALMAE—MY *AUNT*! I WAS STILL HAVING TROUBLE REGISTERING that—had not only taken me to drink a potion, but she also guided me to the kitchen, where I was able to make a sandwich. I had been starving and I hadn't even noticed it.

After, Almae took me to my bedroom on the second floor of the castle. On the way there, we walked by Prince Cain, and I couldn't help but ask how Shane and Twyla were.

"A little tense, but they seemed fine," he said politely. "I've sent food to them, and told them to rest. They will meet with Lord Drake and Queen Thea tomorrow morning to discuss what will happen next."

I thanked him for the information, then let Almae take me the rest of the way.

"This is the guest wing," she said as we walked down a wide corridor with gray stones walls and landscape paintings. Dark archways cut through the corridor every ten feet and two doors.

"I'm in this room." She pointed to a black door to our right. We continued until the next one. "And here is yours."

The suite was huge, even bigger than the one I had with the witches at the lodge. The door opened to a sitting area with a loveseat and side tables. Behind it was an archway that led to the bedroom with a four-poster king-sized bed, a trunk at its foot, two matching nightstands, and a silver-framed full-length mirror in the corner. Then, there were two more doors: a walk-in-closet and a luxurious bathroom with a bathtub for at least five people, a standing shower, and a private toilet.

"This is supposed to be a guest bedroom?" I walked around the bed, touching the gossamer tied to the posts. The furniture was all white, the cushions and bedding were teal and light gray, and the decoration was a mix of metal and glass. Clean, elegant, and expensive looking.

Almae chuckled. "Vampires have a lot of money, and they like to show off."

I turned to her, still taking in all that had happened in so little time. The Nightmist witches, the lies, the second box and Twyla, the warlocks who still kept coming, being in DuMoir Castle, meeting my aunt, and breaking the blood promise.

I glanced at my hands. The blood promise was gone. I now had access to my magic ... well, not right now. My magic was numb because of the potion, and honestly, that made me happy. I didn't want to lose control, because I felt out of place, like I didn't belong.

Belong. Did I belong here? Did I want to belong here? That was another thing for me to figure out.

But I didn't have to do that right now.

I yawned.

Almae showed me a soft smile. "I see you're tired. I'll let you rest. Tomorrow morning, we can have breakfast together and talk more." She walked to me and pulled me into a tight embrace. "I'm so glad I've found you, my dear. Remember, we're family and we'll always be family." She pulled back and looked at me. "Keeran will love having a cousin."

I smiled back. While in the kitchen, she told me about her son—my cousin. Keeran had overthrown Soren as the Warlock Lord, and he was a fair leader. According to her, the warlocks after me weren't associated with Keeran, and because of that, he would be interested in joining us to solve this mystery.

"I'm still shocked, but also glad."

She gave me a kiss on the cheek and patted my shoulder. "Good night, my dear. If you need anything, you know where to find me." She pointed to the right wall, the one my bedroom and hers shared.

"Good night."

She waved at me from the door, then closed it behind her.

Once she left, I went through the motions. I showered, I changed into a silk nightgown I had found in the closet, and I crawled into bed, leaving one of the bedside lamps on.

My body was exhausted and I thought I would crash like a rock.

But I couldn't sleep.

Every new development flooded my mind, making me wide awake.

What would happen to Twyla and Shane? What had happened to the Nightmist witches? Who were the warlocks after me? Would I be able to control my newfound magic? How would I fight the boxes' call? I really hoped Thea and Almae found a way to break my connection to them soon.

And after that, what would happen to me? Would I stay

here? Would they let me stay here? I was practically a Silverblood witch, wasn't I? Would Thea invite me to officially join them? Would I move to their estate?

Restless, I stood up and went to the window. I pushed the curtains open and glanced out. It was full dark now but the moonlight shone bright and illuminated some of the expansive yard below. The castle, the grounds ... everything here seemed out of a fairytale. And I was right in the middle of it all.

This was where Killian had lived for two hundred years. I smiled, thinking of him. I was happy that he had come home, even if it was a little different, and that he would become a prince, as he had always wanted.

A soft knock came from my door.

I turned. Had I imagined it?

The knock came again, and I tiptoed to the sitting room, where I turned on another side lamp.

"I can hear your heartbeat," Killian said, his voice muffled by the door.

I opened the door a crack and spied out. "Hi."

He stood there, his hair damp and wearing clean black slacks and black shirt, and dress shoes. Shit, he cleaned up nicely.

"If you're not too tired, I thought we could talk a bit," he said. "May I come in?"

Aware of my flimsy nightgown, I nodded and opened the door wider—at least it was dim in here.

He walked in, and I closed the door behind him. He stopped in front of the couch in the sitting room, the lamp to his right casting shadows over the sharp angles of his face, and ran a hand through his hair.

I stayed by the door. "Congratulations on becoming a prince."

"Yeah, that. Thank you," he said, sounding halfhearted.

I frowned. "You don't sound excited about it."

"To be honest, I wanted that for so long, but now it doesn't seem that important."

"What could be more important?"

He stared at me, his green eyes darkening. "You."

I inhaled deeply. "Killian ..."

"I need to tell you something, something that I've known for a while and that has been bothering me ever since."

It seemed important. Serious. "Should I sit down for that?"

"It shouldn't be too bad," he said.

I took two steps closer and crossed my arms. "All right. Tell me."

He pressed his lips into a thin line before sighing. "Remember I told you about Sarki? The half-witch, half-vampire who lived here and was a powerful oracle?"

"Was?"

He nodded. "I learned she died several years ago. Anyway, remember I told you she had had two premonitions for me? One was about my brother's death, but I didn't tell you the second. Well, the second was that I would one day find the one who completed me, like ... my soulmate. She said I would know instantly who she was the moment I saw her." He rubbed his hand over his heart. "I would know it right here." He paused. "I felt it the moment I first laid eyes on you."

I gaped at him. Then I frowned, trying to remember the first time he had seen me, when I touched the box and freed him from it. He had attacked me. And then he had stopped. He said, "It's you," and backed away.

I shook my head. "But ..."

"Wait, let me finish," he said in a hurry. "I knew it was you, but you have to put yourself in my shoes. I had loathed and hunted witches for over two hundred years, and then suddenly my soulmate is a freaking witch. I was in denial." His shoulders sagged. "But the more time I spent with you, the more I accepted the idea. The more I liked it. Yes, there were a few days when I was bluntly reminded of what you are, but as the days passed ... that didn't matter much." He clenched his hands. "And then you joined those evil witches, and suddenly, you were one of them. You wanted to stay. It was like a bucket of cold water over my head, waking me up from a dream that could never be."

I could barely breathe. I knew he had been struggling with the fact that I was a witch, but I didn't know it was so bad, so deep. "I apologize for causing you such grief."

Killian scoffed. "The worst part was when you tried leaving, they revealed their lies, and locked you up in that lodge." He took a step closer to me, his eyes pained. "I didn't care anymore. You could have been a ghost, a mummy, an evil siren-slash-mermaid, I didn't care ... I had to help you. I had to save you. I had to make sure you were okay. Because I can't bear it if you're not okay."

My breath hitched. "Killian—"

"One more thing," he interrupted me. "This started as a premonition from an oracle. Soulmates or whatever are predestined. It sounded like we—I—didn't have a choice, but Lavinia ... these feelings are real. They aren't just fate meddling where it shouldn't." He pressed a hand to his heart. "I love you in a way I can't explain." I gasped. "It's deeper and stronger than anything I had ever experienced before." He paused. "I love you, Lavinia." Then he took a step back. "But I know I hurt you. I won't force you to accept this fate, to be with—"

"Oh, shut up," I said, a snarl in my voice that startled even me. "Just shut up and kiss me, you idiot."

His eyes widened for half a second, the corners of his lips tugged up in another half second, and then that was all gone, a pure desire reflected in his eyes as he zoomed into me, slamming his body into mine and winding his arms around my waist to keep me from falling.

"I love you," Killian whispered before lowering his mouth to mine.

I met him halfway. His lips claimed mine and I wrapped my arms around his neck, pulling him closer. The kiss started slow, sensual, but soon the rhythm of his mouth on mine intensified. The kiss went faster and deeper. His hands slid down around my butt, and down my thighs. Supported by his hands, I lifted my legs and clamped them around his waist. Without breaking the delicious kiss, Killian backed us up to the wall. He pushed me into the wall, pressing his hips against mine. I gasped in his mouth, feeling his hard-on. Oh God, I needed him, I needed him right now.

Killian snaked his hands under my nightgown, skimming the skin of my thighs, sending shivers up my spine. I expected his hands to be cold, but they weren't too bad. Actually, they felt like a balm on my suddenly too hot skin.

Breaking the kiss, Killian gently dropped me and turned me around. I braced myself on the wall, as he slid one hand around my breasts and another continued its path around my thighs. I moved my hips, rubbing my ass on his hard-on.

"Oh, shit," he whispered, his mouth near my ear.

I pulled my hair to the side and stretched my neck. "Bite me," I told him.

Killian stilled. He pulled back a little and looked into my eyes. "Are you sure?"

I nodded.

Slowly, he lowered his head to my neck and dragged his lips over my skin. The anticipation built and I groaned. Knowing exactly what he was doing to me, Killian pinched my nipple and slid his hand lower, under my panties.

Oh God.

I felt the tip of his fangs right before he bit me. At the same time, he pinched my nipple again and slid a finger inside me.

Oh God.

The desire exploded like fireworks in my veins, in my core, in every inch of my body. Thank goodness Killian was strong, because my knees buckled and I would have fallen if he hadn't kept me up, somehow. He drank my blood slowly, sending whatever it was into me, building up the desire, the ecstasy. He rubbed his thumb over my clit and slid another finger inside me, pumping fast and hard.

"Oh God," I whispered, knowing I was losing. I wanted more, I wanted to hang on, but I couldn't. This was too much. I was drowning in too much pleasure.

Killian clasped his hand around my entire breast, holding me tight against him. His bite, his fingers, his hand, his hard-on against my ass ... I cried out as the climax hit me like a bomb and I exploded in a million shivers.

Gently, Killian pulled back his fingers and retracted his fangs. As I trembled in his arms, he kissed my neck.

Still flying high, I took control. I turned around, slipped my panties off, and reached for his pants and undid the button. One corner of Killian's lips curled up as he helped me. A second later, his pants were gone, and I braced my back on the wall and wrapped my legs around his waist again.

"Come here," I said, almost commanding.

"My pleasure," Killian said, stepping closer, caging me against the wall again.

I grasped his shoulders for balance and moved my hips, lining us up perfectly. Killian groaned as he slowly slid into me. My breath caught as he buried himself deep, filling me completely. Oh God, he was so big, so thick ...

I moved again, wiggling my hips. "Please."

"Holy shit," he whispered, pressing his lips against mine and finally moving his hips. Out and in, out and in. I moaned as pleasure like I never knew existed coursed through me in tidal waves.

But beyond the pleasure, I felt something else, something warm and tender in my chest, a band tightening against my heart, an invisible cord that stretched out ... toward Kilian's chest.

"Do you feel this?" he asked, breaking the kiss and stopping. I nodded. "It's the mating bond."

I stared at him. "Like ..." I had seen this in movies, mostly, and it usually happened to shifters.

"Like a soulmate's bond," he said. The cord stretched even more, and then it snapped taught, tugging at my heart. Killian gasped. "It's done." His eyes searched mine. "You're really my soulmate." Then he started moving again and brought his lips to mine. "I knew it," he muttered against my lips.

My head was slow to catch up, but right now I didn't care.

I was in Killian's arms, feeling like I never had before, and from what I gathered he was mine and I was his.

Perfection.

With a snarl, Killian locked an arm around my waist and moved us to my bed. He gently sat me down, then peeled off my nightgown. I scooted to the middle of the bed, my eyes on his and his eyes on me, as he took off his shirt.

I bit down on my lower lip as I took him in—all hard and lean muscle and ... Good lord, how did he fit inside me?

He crawled in bed over me. "You're so beautiful," he said as he lowered his body to mine. "So, so beautiful." Killian slid inside me again. "And so tight, and so wet. Holy shit."

I moaned as he started moving and Killian silenced me with a kiss. He assaulted my mouth, robbing me of air, and I reached around his shoulders, gently scratching my nails on his skin, over the many dips and lines of his muscles.

Like this, naked with his skin, his entire body rubbing against mine, it was even better. He went oh so deep, and the line between pain and pure pleasure blurred. It felt too good. This ecstasy, this passion ... it built up to dangerous levels.

I moved my lips around his jaw and whispered in his ear, "I love you too."

"Shit." He groaned and sank even deeper into me. Moving faster and faster, he brought his lips to mine again and kissed me.

This ... there was nothing like this. I'd had sex before, but this was different. This was making love, but supercharged. Making love with my soulmate. The desire shot through my veins, my belly tightened, and I couldn't hold anymore.

I cried as I came again.

Killian thrust two more times, then broke out in trembles. He pressed his head to my neck as he rode the ecstasy. A few seconds later, he lifted himself on his elbows and looked at me. "I love you."

I smiled. "You already said that."

"Get used to it. I'll say it all the time."

"Good." I reached up and placed a peck on his lips. He settled over me, his face on my neck, his body over mine—though I knew he was bearing most of his weight—and I wound my arms and legs around him again. "I want to stay like this. Forever."

"I have no objections," he mumbled, his lips moving against my skin.

I held on to him, feeling light and happy, despite everything else looming over us.

With Killian by my side, I knew everything would be okay.

29

———

WHEN KILLIAN WOKE UP AND SAID HE HAD TO MEET WITH Lord Drake, I held on to him. I wanted to live in our quiet bubble for a few more hours. Here, we could pretend it was just us, that we were Killian and Lavinia, and that no danger lurked over our heads.

But nothing lasted forever.

Though now I knew my love for Killian would.

We were freaking soulmates! Last night, when we were tangled together, resting after the most wonderful time, Killian explained to me that it was rare for vampires to have mates. It was more of a shifter thing. So, the fact that we had found each other was not only fate, but a miracle.

He also told me that when he lived here, the castle operated on an opposite schedule—day was night, and night was day, since vampires were a little more sensitive to sunlight. But yesterday he learned DuMoir Castle now followed a normal schedule, and he thought it was because of the witches. To me, that spelled love—it had been Drake's love for Thea that had made him change it.

I watched from the bed, wrapped in the bedsheets, as he got dressed. He stopped in front of the full-length mirror and ran a hand through his hair.

"Did I tell you you're hot?" I asked, suddenly horny again. We had made love not once, but twice last night, and he had told me he loved at least three more times. And I had replied, "Keep acting like a freaking model in front of me and I won't let you leave this room."

Killian turned to me, a real smile on his lips. I gasped, surprised by it. I had never seen him smile, and holy shit, he was even more handsome.

He braced himself on the bed, leaned into me, and pressed his lips to mine. "I know you also have to meet Thea and Acalla, er, Almae, soon." He shook his head. "I still can't believe she's your aunt."

"Me neither." What were the odds my aunt was the one who created the boxes and helped put him inside one of them? I knew she hadn't had a choice, but I also knew Killian resented her for it.

He placed a soft kiss on my shoulder. "Meet me for lunch?"

I arched an eyebrow. "Back here? So we can continue this?" I gestured between him and me.

That earned me another dazzling smile. Oh my heart. "Who are you and what have you done with my soulmate?"

I chuckled. "Your soulmate didn't know what love really was and now she's kind of addicted to it."

He pressed his lips to my neck. "I know. It's hard to leave you, trust me, but there are important things that need our attention. Besides ..." He kissed my jaw. "We can continue this tonight, for sure."

"I'm counting on it." I turned my face so his lips lined

with mine. Killian cupped my face and kissed me—deep and hard, but way too short.

He pulled back and rested his forehead on mine. "During lunch, we should talk."

I tensed. "What's the matter now?"

"Once, you asked me what it was like inside the box. I think ... I think I'm ready to tell you. You're my soulmate. You should know everything about me."

Holding the bedsheets around me, I sat up and pressed a hand to his heart. Though I knew this would probably be painful for him, I was glad he wanted to tell me. "And I'm ready to listen."

On a lighter note, Killian hooked one finger around the bedsheet and tugged it down. He groaned, before claiming my mouth again. "I really should go," he whispered against my lips. I scooted closer. "Damn it, woman." He broke the kiss. "If I don't go now, I'm not leaving, so ..." He placed another soft kiss on my nose and I smiled, triumphant. "I'm out." He walked to the archway dividing the bedroom from the sitting room and paused. "I'll see you later."

I nodded.

He marched to the door and disappeared beyond it.

I stayed in bed for a few more minutes, enjoying the moment. The bedsheets and pillows smelled of Killian—it was hard for me to even let those go.

A smile adorned my lips. Killian was my soulmate. He had tried denying it because I was a witch, but he had come to love me despite that. And I loved him. Right now, right here in this bubble, life was perfect.

I only got up and got dressed to meet with Almae and Thea because I knew that tonight after the ceremony to make him a prince, Killian and I would return to our bubble.

I had seen everyone dressed in tailored suits in this castle, even the few females I had seen, so I ended up ditching my jeans for a black pantsuit I found in the closet, along with a white blouse and black pumps. I felt like a fish out of water, but I didn't want to draw unwanted attention to myself. Once I was more comfortable in this place, with the people living here, I would rethink my wardrobe.

Living here ...

Would I live here? I mean, after last night, I guess I wouldn't go anywhere without Killian, and if he stayed here, so would I, right?

I frowned as I combed my hair in front of the mirror.

Well, we hadn't talked about that, but it was clear to me that Killian and I were a thing now. We wouldn't be separated anymore, no matter what happened.

Right?

My stomach growled. It seemed that was my cue to find breakfast. I grabbed my phone from the nightstand and I headed for the door, but paused in the sitting room. I glanced to the bedroom, thinking of the closet. My bag was in there, and in my bag were my dagger and my flashlight. Should I take them with me?

I shook my head, feeling silly. There was no reason for me to walk around the castle with those, especially the dagger.

Lighter and more confident than I had felt in ages, I walked out of my bedroom. I knocked on Almae's door, but she didn't answer. I frowned, wondering what I should do. Wait for her to get me, or walk until I bumped into someone who could point me to either the kitchen—I had been there last night, but this castle was huge and I didn't know the way by heart yet—or to Almae.

I decided on the latter.

I trudged along the corridor Almae and I had come from, and turned right at an intersection. I went for several steps, then stopped, confused. Shouldn't I have arrived at the stairs already? I turned back and—

A gloved hand closed around my mouth and nose, and an arm locked around my waist.

Fear rushed through me, and I screamed against the hand, but it was muffled. I jerked against the hold, and dropped my phone with the effort, but whoever was holding me was too strong.

"Stop, bitch," a voice said, right beside my ear.

I inhaled—what an odd scent.

It hit me then. It wasn't a glove, it was a rag and it was damp with valerian and something else I couldn't tell. I stopped breathing, but it was probably too late. I shook my shoulders and kicked my legs.

"I said stop it."

Something slammed into the back of my head and stars exploded in my vision.

No, no, no … This couldn't be happening, not now.

My magic! I now had my full magic! I called my powers … but they didn't answer. The potion Almae gave me last night must still be working, because even though I was in danger, I couldn't even access a drop of it.

Oh, shit.

My legs and arms weighed like anchors. I blinked, trying hard not to sleep. But it was to no avail.

"There you go," the voice said as my body became limb. "Good night, bitch."

Darkness enveloped me and I fell into a deep slumber.

WAS I DEAD?

No, death couldn't hurt this much.

My brain was foggy, but my muscles ached as I tried to move. Tried ... I jerked in a hard bed, but could barely move an inch. I fought against the dizziness in my mind, and spied under my lashes for a second—all I saw was darkness. Panic rose inside me along with something else, a discomfort in my stomach, a wave of nausea ... holy shit.

I rolled up to the side before I became sick over myself, but still couldn't move.

Pushing through the fog, I snapped my eyes closed.

Shadows shifted in the darkness, some with sharp teeth, some with brilliant eyes, and some with long claws. They all danced around me as if taunting me, making me more scared before actually attacking.

It was working.

"She's delirious," a voice said.

"It's just a side effect. I'll pass soon."

Was that ... the shadows? I glanced around. More shadows hovered closer. My panic increased.

I closed my eyes again and breathed through my mouth, trying to control my emotions, the sudden shivering of my body, the dizziness in my brain.

But tied like this and in the darkness, there wasn't much I could do.

The pain and the nausea got worse, before finally, after an eternity, it got better. Next time I opened my eyes, the shadows were gone, but I was still in a dark room, and I was cuffed to what felt like a stone bed, with four men looming over me.

"She's awake," one of them said. He touched my arm. I jerked on instinct, but my arm didn't move. He fussed with something on my inner elbow. An IV.

"What the ...?" My chest seized. "What is this? What's going on? Who are you?"

Dim light shone from somewhere in the distance, and the fogginess in my mind turned into a dull pain in the back of my eyes.

"Relax, Lavinia," one of the men said, his voice detached. "It'll be over soon."

I groaned as the pain and the nausea assaulted me again, stronger this time. I wanted to tell him to go to hell, but I knew that if I opened my mouth, I would throw up.

For a moment, all I could do was stay quiet and focus on the light shining behind the men, but then something pushed into my arm through the IV, a thick liquid that burned like fire—and magic.

I gasped as magic that wasn't my own filled my veins. The nausea came back, and I gritted my teeth and inhaled deeply through my nose. It wasn't working.

A few seconds or an eternity later, a man said, "It's done."

The IV was gone and the cuffs around my arms and legs were undone. I rolled to my side, and fell from the bed onto my hands and knees on a cold, stone floor. Pain jolted through my limb as I dry-heaved, but nothing came out ... how long had it been since I had last eaten?

It had been ... with Almae, at DuMoir Castle. I stilled. Killian, my bedroom, the hallway, someone attacked me.

Panic tightened in my gut. I pushed up to my wobbly feet and leaned against the stone bed—no, not a bed. A heavy table with a stone top.

I stared at the four men, now standing to one side of the table, watching me. They varied in shape, height, and color, but they all wore black clothing and black capes fell from their shoulders.

Warlocks.

Oh, shit.

Instantly, I called my magic. The effect of the numbing tea Almae had given me was gone, right? How long had it been since then? I felt immense magic filling my veins, more than I had ever imagined I could have before, and threw my hands at them.

My magic sparked, like a failed firework, and exploded in my face. I yelped and leaned farther over the table.

What the hell was that?

I tried again, but the same thing happened. It was like my magic died once it left my hands.

The warlocks snickered.

"What did you do to me?" I barked as I called my magic again.

"Don't bother attacking us," a warlock said. "You won't be able to."

"We gave you a potion that makes your power pliable," another one said.

"Which means, you can't use your magic against us," a third one said.

I stared at my hands. No, that wasn't possible. Stubborn, I tried it again. And the same happened. The magic fizzled out as soon as it left my hand and small sparks flashed in front of me.

My stomach contracted, queasier than before. I pressed a hand over it.

"You should stop before you get hurt."

I glared at the warlocks, at the moment more angry than scared. What the hell had they done to me? I now had magic and couldn't use it against them? How was that possible? Despite the questions swirling in my mind, I held my tongue.

Except for one.

"Where am I?" I looked around the large room. It seemed like a lab of sorts, like the Nightmist's potion room and Thea's workroom—with some work tables, herbs, crystals, and tools used in an apothecary.

"Oh, where are my manners." A warlock with dark skin and sleek black hair to his shoulders stepped closer. On instinct, I matched it and stepped back, but my back pressed to the table behind me. I had nowhere to go.

"I'm Eldon, Warlock Lord of the Red Moon Villa." He gestured to the others. "This is Tack."

"We've met before," Tack said. My eyes widened as I recognized him. He had been the one who attacked Killian and me at the inn two or three weeks ago. I had lost track of time. He was taller than me, but not the tallest here, and his short hair was the color of salt and pepper. "Nice to see you again."

"It's a shame I didn't finish you back then," I said between gritted teeth. I had attacked him with my magic, but it had been weak and it had put him down temporarily.

Tack didn't seem one bit fazed.

A short and mostly bald warlock lifted his hand in hello. "I'm Damien." I stared at him. What? Did he expect me to wave back at him?

"And I'm Bates," said the fourth one, his tone quiet. He was tall and lean and a little younger than the others. Unlike the others, he didn't hold my gaze long. In fact, he seemed to want to look everywhere but at me.

I frowned. Why did that name ring a bell?

"There are some things you should understand, Lavinia," Eldon said, drawing my attention back to him. "First, you can't use your magic against us. Second is that there's no way out of here. And third, you'll end up helping us, even if you don't want to." His lips stretched into a wicked, closed smile.

I shuddered.

"But please, put up a fight," Damien said, a naughty glint in his dark eyes. "It'll be fun if you do."

The nausea in my stomach increased.

Eldon clicked his tongue. "That's enough for now. Tack, take her to her bedroom."

Without ceremony, Tack advanced and closed a hand around my upper arm. I jerked against him, but he was stronger than me. I could fight more, but what was the point? He was visibly stronger, there were four of them against one of me, and I couldn't use my magic to save my life.

I was doomed.

Tack pulled me close and leaned over. "Yes, *please*, misbehave. We will love to have a reason to play with you." Despite myself, I shuddered again. His grip around my arm tightened and he tugged me forward. "Now, let's go, witch."

"Wait." My step faltered. I looked from Tack to Eldon. I needed to ask them something, even though I was sure I knew the answer. I had to hear it from their own lips. "Why am I here?"

Eldon's lips peeled back, showing his wicked grin. "To collect the boxes and finish the spell. And *you* will help me."

CONTINUE LAVINIA+KILLIAN'S adventure with *The Darkest Magic*, book 3 in the Rite World: Vampire Wars series!

Did you like Evelyn and Asher? They have their own book about how they met, called *The Light Witch,* and you can find it in my Facebook group, Juliana's Club! Join and find this free and exclusive book in the Featured tab! ;)

Curious about the Rite World universe? Check out this page on my website. It has the recommended reading order and links to grab more books!

THANK YOU

Thank you for reading *The Darkest Witch*!

Reviews are very important for authors. If you liked my book, please consider leaving a review on your favorite online retailer and/or on Goodreads and/or Bookbub, please!

Don't forget to pre-order the next book in the series, *The Darkest Magic!*

Did you like this book? You can check out other books of mine:

The Midnight Test (Rite World: Lightgrove Witches 1): a clueless witch is invited to join a powerful coven—but only if she aces a difficult test.

The Demon Kiss (Rite World: Blackthorn Hunters Academy book 1): a fast-paced story about a young woman who finds out she's a demon hunter, and the half-demon intent on protecting her against all evil.

The Vampire Heir (Rite World 1: Rite of the Vampire): a dark and mysterious paranormal romance about a vampire and a young woman with a secret.

The Warlock Lord (Rite World 4: Rite of the Warlock): a thrilling and kick-ass paranormal romance about a werewolf and warlock.

The Wolf Forsaken (Rite World 7: Rite of the Wolf): a heat-wrenching tale about a lost wolf shifter and a fae princess on the run.

Heart Seeker (The Fire Heart Chronicles book 1): an urban fantasy series about a young woman who finds herself at the center of a mysterious supernatural world.

Destiny Gift (The Everlast Series book 1): a post-apocalyptic urban fantasy series about a young woman with a special power that can save the world.

DON'T FORGET to sign up for my Newsletter to find out about new releases, cover reveals, giveaways, and more!

If you want to see exclusive teasers, help me decide on covers, read excerpts, talk about books, etc, join my reader group on Facebook: Juliana's Club!

ABOUT THE AUTHOR

While USA Today Bestselling Author Juliana Haygert dreams of being Wonder Woman, Buffy, or a blood elf shadow priest, she settles for the less exciting—but equally gratifying—life as a wife, a mother, and an author. She resides in North Carolina and spends her days writing about kick-ass heroines and the heroes who drive them crazy.

Subscribe to her mailing list to receive emails of announcement, events, and other fun stuff related to her writing and her books: www.bit.ly/JuHNL

For more information:
www.julianahaygert.com

facebook.com/julianahaygert

twitter.com/julianahaygert

instagram.com/juliana.haygert

goodreads.com/juliana_haygert

pinterest.com/julianahaygert

bookbub.com/authors/juliana-haygert

youtube.com/julianahaygert

patreon.com/julianahaygert

ALSO BY JULIANA HAYGERT

To find links and more info, go to:

www.julianahaygert.com/books/

Shorts

Into the Darkest Fire

Standalones

Daughter of Darkness

Rite World: Vampire Wars

The Darkest Vampire (Book 1)

The Darkest Witch (Book 2)

The Darkest Magic (Book 3)

Rite World: Lightgrove Witches

The Midnight Test (Book 1)

The Midnight Spell (Book 2)

The Midnight Flame (Book 3)

Rite World: Blackthorn Hunters Academy

The Demon Kiss (Book 1)

The Hunter Secret (Book 2)

The Soul Bond (Book 3)

The Shadow Trials (Book 4)

The Infernal Curse (Book 5)

Rite World

The Vampire Heir (Book 1)

The Witch Queen (Book 2)

The Immortal Vow (Book 3)

The Warlock Lord (Book 4)

The Wolf Consort (Book 5)

The Crystal Rose (Book 6)

The Wolf Forsaken (Book 7)

The Fae Bound (Book 8)

The Blood Pact (Book 9)

The Wyth Courts

Winter King (Book 1)

Spring Warrior (Book 2)

Summer Prince (Book 3)

Autumn Rebel (Book 4)

The Fire Heart Chronicles

Heart Seeker (Book 1)

Flame Caster (Book 2)

Earth Shaker (Book 2.5)

Sorrow Bringer (Book 3)

Soul Wanderer (Book 4)

Fate Summoner (Book 5)

War Maiden (Book 6)